The Vow

Milton M. Smilek

CROSSBOOKS
PUBLISHING

CrossBooks™
A Division of LifeWay
1663 Liberty Drive
Bloomington, IN 47403
www.crossbooks.com
Phone: 1-866-879-0502

First published by CrossBooks 12/23/2011

ISBN: 978-1-4627-1130-7 (sc)
ISBN: 978-1-4627-1132-1 (hc)
ISBN: 978-1-4627-1131-4 (e)

Library of Congress Control Number: 2011918281

Printed in the United States of America

This book is printed on acid-free paper.

To my wife MaryAnn

FORWARD

"It's quite a lovely love story"

Lori Handelman, Phd., Editorial Consulting
Clear Voice Editing

PREFACE

Our way of life is constantly changing and is very different from the life our forefathers knew, but their sayings, their moral teachings and their words of wisdom have not. Their morale teachings are applicable today as they were yesterday and will be tomorrow. What is morally correct does not change, it is we who change.

Thanks to Ted Kelly and his wife Bonnie, for it was their inspiration which encouraged me to write. The book they were referring to was one based on police stories I would tell while vacationing in Italy. Perhaps that might be a good idea for the next book.

Thanks to John Krieger and his wife Lori who also encouraged me, and thanks to all four of them for listening to my chatter, and offering their constructive criticisms.

Thanks to Don Commerford, who did the final grammatical proof of this book, and wrote on the last page- thank you.

Introduction

If you want to learn what the term "Family Values" really means – then read this story.

A young boy grew up amidst the life struggles of an immigrant culture in America. The joys of love and success are intertwined with the pains of death and heartache.

Follow the drama and lessons learned alongside the tensions of being different in an American neighborhood. Young and old alike can appreciate what's really correct as seen and told through the skillfully written lines. The beauty of love isn't hidden anywhere, but the reader is regularly balanced by ideals and values more treasured than love's derived physically or emotional appeal. A good read.

John Krieger

I think this is an excellent book, a good old fashioned love story intertwined with many of the issues we are facing today. The story takes many twist and turns, and the ending will surprise you.

Ted Kelly

CHAPTER ONE

"The Beautiful Island"

⚜ January temperatures vary around the mid-eighties, but today was a very warm day and Dad was very deep in thought. As he sat in his office, he wondered the outcome of the war. He also wondered if there was anything he could do to help. Dad, Angel Herera, was a handsome man with straight blond hair, light green eyes, and a light sun-kissed complexion. He was tall for a Hispanic, with the build of an athlete.

Our mom, Maria, was just as beautiful as Dad was handsome. She had long, pitch-black hair, brown deep-set eyes, a light complexion, and a medium build.

They were very much in love. They had met during their senior year at San German University, and after a two-year courtship, they married in February of 1932. They had three gorgeous children, Manuel who was born in May of 1934, Lucy born in April of 1936, and me, Anthony. I was born in November of 1938. One could say we had an ideal family. My father was a civil engineer for the city of San German, Puerto Rico. We lived in the suburbs of San German in a large house with a spectacular view of the countryside. Judging by the standards of our time, one could consider us to be financially well-off, and very happy.

Today, Father was frustrated. He personally did not know the cause of his frustration, but had a deep inner feeling he had to do something. *He*

1

was a people person, and often spent his time helping others. Somehow, he felt he had to do more, but was uncertain of what.

He arrived home and Mom greeted him at the door, as she has done on many occasions. However, today she had a strange feeling that something was wrong. It was then that Dad told her he was going to enlist in the United States Army. Mom asked him if he had been working in the sun. Dad told her he was very serious. He told her he wanted to do something for his country, besides he was upset at the Japanese for attacking Pearl Harbor, and detested Hitler and his policy.

Dad loved his freedom and was willing to sacrifice his life, so we could be able to enjoy that same freedom. Mom saw in his eyes that he was serious, so she brought the children into the conversation. It was fruitless, because it appeared Dad's mind had been made up. Dad stated, "I am going to see the recruiter in the morning."

Mom could not sleep that night. She laid in bed thinking about what she would do if something should happen to her wonderful husband she deeply loved.

All night she pondered her approach on how to convince him to change his mind. Her plan was to bring the matter up in the morning before Dad left to see the recruiter. She would try the, "Don't you love me anymore?" approach. Early the next morning, Mom implemented her plan. She began by asking Dad, "Don't you love me anymore, that you want to leave me? What about our children, don't you love them either? How would we survive without you?" Everything she tried failed.

Dad's mind had been made up. All that Mom could do at this point was to pray that he would somehow change his mind.

During the latter part of 1942, Dad departed for his Basic Military Training. Upon completion of his training, he was shipped overseas and found himself in the middle of a battlefield in a strange country.

One evening the gunfire and the explosions appeared to be heavier. On that evening, as numerous shots rang out, Dad felt a burning sensation deep inside the right side of his head. At first he was not sure of what had happened. He thought it might be a headache coming on.

His vision became blurry. He felt a slight dizziness, and a warm sweat running down the side of his head. He wiped the sweat and looked at his hand; it was then that panic set in. He realized it was his blood -- he had been shot.

Dad's first thought was, "Oh Lord I can't die, I have three small children, I can't do this to my wife. I love them all very much, and I promised them I would return home safely." The last thing he saw was the images of our faces before he lost consciousness. Dad woke up several weeks later in Walter Reed Army Hospital. The doctors told him he had some brain damage, and as a result a plate had been implanted in his head. They also told him he would be released on a medical discharge, which would include a monthly disability check.

Dad knew that the disability income would not be enough money to raise his family the way he wanted. He asked himself, "Did I do the right thing by enlisting, was my wife right when she told me not to enlist? What would I tell her, how could I make it up to her and my children?" Dad was reunited with us, and after several months we were forced to rent our house and move in with Dad's parents in Sabana Grande, P.R. The reason for the move was strictly financial.

We now had to compensate for Dad's new and much lower income. Due to Dad's injuries, he was unable to return to his prior employment. In fact, he had difficulty obtaining any job because his injuries were apparent in his speech and his demeanor.

On occasions, he would slur his words, and had difficulty keeping his mind on the present subject. Sometimes, under stressful situations, his mind would wander and he would babble, making no sense at all. In addition, he had constant migraine headaches.

Living with the in-laws was very difficult for Mom. Dad's mother would take care of Dad as though he was her young son who had returned home. She catered to Dad, and treated Mom as if she was an outsider.

She liked Manuel and Lucy, but treated me the same way she treated Mom. I believe it was because I looked like and reminded her of Mom. Mom further thought her mother-in-law was blaming her for what happened to Dad.

It came to the point that Mom talked to her mother-in-law about the way she and I were being treated. Dad's mother responded by telling her, "It's just your imagination."

Mom decided to leave and go to America, where she would get a job and save enough money to bring all of us to live with her. Mom believed in America we could start a new life.

Mom felt it would be all right for Lucy and Manuel to stay with Dad at his parent's house, but felt it would be better for me to go live with her parents in the rural area of San German, P.R.

She was afraid that her mother-in-law would continue to treat me as though I was inferior to my brother and sister, possibly causing me to develop psychological problems. A week later, Mom took me to live with her parents, and left for America.

Mom's parents were somewhat poor, but very happy. They lived in a rural area, and their house was an old wood frame house, with three bedrooms, a big kitchen, a large parlor, a front porch and a tin roof. During the rainy season you could hear the heavy rain softly ringing on the roof top.

They had what they needed. They had each other, a solid roof over their heads, and plenty of good food to eat. They had no running water inside their house, so fresh water was brought into the house from the community well.

In order to bathe, we would walk to the nearby river or to the common community well. At the common community well, there was an overhead shower where one could wash. However, one had to wear a bathing suit, or proper bathing attire.

The old house had electricity. There were three electric wires hanging from the ceiling, one in the kitchen, one in the parlor, and the other on the front porch. Each hanging wire contained a pull chain. The pull chains were used to light a bulb which was screwed into the pull chain socket. The rest of the rooms were lit by candle light.

There were three wires which contained outlets. One was used for a fan, the other for the radio, and the third was a spare.

Mom's parents considered themselves to be very fortunate, because they had three cows, six pigs, over thirty chickens, six roosters, and three goats, animals that on many occasions I would look after.

In the United States, Mom stayed with her cousin Anna, who lived in the Chelsea section of New York City. She obtained a job working in a large restaurant cooking Spanish dishes. Her goal was to make enough money to bring Dad, Lucy, Manny, and me to the United States. Mom believed the United States was the place she planned to spend the rest of her life.

Mom also believed that America would be the place where we could receive a better education, have more economic opportunities, and a place where our lives would drastically improve. Mom would also try to obtain better medical treatment for Dad. She was optimistic that something could be done to help him.

Manuel and Lucy missed their mom, but they had Dad and each other. However, I felt very sad and lonely. I would often cry in my bed during the evening hours. I felt as though I had been abandoned. Not only was I in a new environment, I also missed my family. Most importantly I missed my father. I felt as if no one cared for me. *We all try to find someone in our lives we can look up to. Someone we can always depend upon, one who is trustworthy, consistent, and would be there for us no matter what types of problems we may be going through.*

When we find the right person, we try to emulate them, perhaps make them our confidant, and share with them our innermost secrets. Many times we go to them for advice and help. We call them our heroes.

To me, my father was my hero. I was not aware of how serious his injuries were. If I had known, it would not change my feelings toward him. My father would still remain my hero. My father would try to visit me as often as he could. I enjoyed my father's company, and couldn't wait for his next visit. During one visit, he promised me that on his next trip he would bring me my favorite goat cheese.

Dad did visit me on the next scheduled date; however, he arrived late and I was already asleep. It was best for me because, due to his mental state, he forgot to bring me the goat cheese he had promised.

On Dad's next visit, I asked him why he didn't visit me last week. Dad told me he had arrived late, and that I was already asleep. I asked Dad about the goat cheese, and he told me he had brought the cheese, but the cat had gotten a hold of it and ate it.

Shortly before Christmas, during one of Dad's visits, he asked me what I wanted for Christmas. I told him I wanted a guitar. In Puerto Rico, Christmas is celebrated on the arrival of the Three Wise Men (Three Kings), which occurs during the early part of January.

The idea of Santa Claus did not exist. Instead, The Wise Men, who traveled on camels, would bring the children gifts. The children would leave cocoa for The Wise Men to drink, and small, neatly-tied bundles of straw and water for the camels to eat and drink. Christmas came and went and I did not see my father, nor did I receive the guitar he had promised me.

My first lesson on love came at a very young age. It all began shortly after Christmas of 1948, when I was just ten years old. I had been living with my grandparents for the past four years, and had become close to my two cousins, who lived very close to us. There was Ricky, who was two years older than I, and Angelo, who was three years older.

One day I was telling my cousins how wonderful my father was. Ricky asked me why I thought my father was so wonderful. I told him that my father would bring me my favorite goat cheese when he would visit.

I continued to tell them how just recently my father brought me cheese, but that the family cat had eaten it. Ricky told me, "You're a liar, your cat doesn't eat cheese, your father never brought you that cheese."

The next time the family had my favorite goat cheese, I offered a small piece to the cat, the cat smelled it, and walked away without eating it. I wanted to believe my father had brought me the cheese. I then remembered that my father never visited me for Christmas, nor did he bring me the guitar he had promised. I was deeply saddened and my eyes filled with tears.

I began to evaluate my life to see if I had done anything wrong. Perhaps I did something wrong to hurt my father, something that would prevent him from visiting me.

I deeply loved my father, but I began to question his love for me. I asked myself, "Why am I living with my grandparents, and my brother and sister are living with Dad?"

My grandfather and I became very close and loved each other very much. To me, my grandfather became my second father. As a child I usually stated what was on my mind, and my grandfather was always there to listen and give me advice.

On the other hand, my two cousins were always teasing me. I, being younger and more gullible, was an easy target for them.

I approached my grandfather that evening and relayed to him the goat cheese incident, and how my father didn't visit me or bring me anything for Christmas. My grandfather told me about the wounds my father had received while defending our country.

He also told me that my father was a very good man and loved me very much, but because of his head injuries, at times he would forget things. My grandfather said, *"We have to give people a chance in life, and not judge them until they have a chance to explain themselves." Grandfather continued, "The Indians have a saying, which is not to judge others until you have walked a mile in their moccasins."*

I asked Grandfather to explain what that saying meant. He told me, "We do not know what a person's personal problems may be, or what they are going through in life. Sometimes things happen in their lives, and they are forced to make decisions we may not understand. Once we find out more about them and what they have experienced, perhaps then we can have a better idea of why they make certain decisions."

My grandfather told me, "Ask your father any question you might have on your mind on his next visit." Grandfather assured me that my father would have a good explanation.

A few days later, my grandfather received a message from my other grandfather. The message was that my father had passed away as a result of his war injuries, and that the funeral would be tomorrow.

My grandfather gently told me the news of my father's passing. I felt a pain in my gut, and was saddened. I could not cry because all I could think of was, "I will never find out why my father had not visited me for Christmas. Why he had not brought me the guitar he had promised, or will I ever know if he really loved me?" Then the tears came.

The custom in Puerto Rico is to have a one-day wake service in the family home. This usually takes place in the parlor, or in some cases the largest room in the house. The body is then taken to the church for the funeral services. Afterwards, it is taken to the cemetery for interment.

Only the very rich could afford the services of a funeral parlor, where the body would be embalmed, a two- or three-day wake service would be held, followed by the church service and interment.

Grandfather could not telephone Mom to tell her the news of Dad's passing. Both Mom and my grandparents had no access to a telephone. Grandfather sent Mom a telegraph, hoping she would receive it in time. Grandfather, in the past, had bad experiences with the telegraph company, so he also wrote Mom a letter. He believed the best way to communicate was by mail.

Mom received the telegraph and the letter of Dad's death on the same day. They were both brought to Mom by her cousin Anna. Mom read the letter from her hospital bed.

She felt a deep pain in her heart. She had no idea that her husband was that ill. In his last letter she believed he was feeling much better, and was looking forward to his move to America, where they would spend the rest of their lives together.

Tears filled her eyes. When Mom received the letter of Dad's death, he had already been buried. She was very sad that she could not be there to say goodbye to the man she loved and admired so much. Mom had just undergone surgery to have her appendix removed. When she cried it would hurt her side, but she couldn't control her emotions.

Grandfather took the family to the funeral services. We had no vehicle, so we hired a   Publico (a privately owned public taxi). On the way to the funeral, my grandfather used the opportunity to explain to me the meaning of death. He said, "Death is our final destination, a much better place called heaven, where there is no pain, no suffering, no sorrow and it is full of happiness and joy."

He continued, "There we would be reunited with our families, our friends, and most importantly, with the Lord." Grandfather also told me, "In order to get there you would have to live a good life, one which included having the Lord as your close friend."

I asked Grandfather, "Did my father have a good relationship with Jesus?" His reply was, "Your father was a good man, and had a wonderful relationship with the Lord."

Many family members and friends attended the funeral. At the funeral I thought how I would miss my father's visits. So what if he didn't love me, we played games and had a lot of fun together when he visited me.

After the funeral everyone was invited to my father's parent's house for the repast. After lunch, both my grandfathers took me to my father's room.

Here, my father's dad told me, "I have something to give you, something your father asked me to give to you if anything should happen to him. He had just finished making it and was going to give it to you for Christmas before he got severely ill."

He brought out a very beautiful guitar. My eyes began to fill with tears, not because the guitar was so beautiful, nor because my father had made it especially for me, but because I knew my father loved me.

I realized my grandfather had been right. *I should not have judged my Father, until I knew more about his situation, his intentions, or perhaps given him a chance to explain his feelings.* This made my day; I was at peace with myself and with my father.

Several days later I received a letter from Mom, which stated she would be coming to visit us at the end of the month, which was about three weeks away. In the same letter she also told me to have my bags packed because she would be taking all of us back to the United States to live with her.

I waited anxiously for Mom's arrival, and to pass time, my two cousins and I would hunt grouse in our wooded/semi-jungle backyard. We would hunt grouse with slingshots.

Grouse are very fast and alert birds, and are very difficult to hunt, especially with a slingshot. It was even more difficult for me, because I made a lot of noise and would scare them. Also, my aim was horrendous.

I was such a poor shot that my cousins would make fun of me. They teased me so much that at times I would have tears in my eyes, tears I would hide from them.

One day, after a hunt, I was alone with my grandfather. Grandfather knew that something was bothering me, so he sat next to me and asked me why I was so gloomy.

I told him that I was a failure, because everything I attempted would often fail. To make things worse, I was often teased for my mistakes. I also told him of my bad hunting abilities, and how terrible I was shooting a slingshot.

Grandfather told me, *"Sometimes we fail at things, but we have to get back on our feet and try again and try harder."* Grandfather gave me some tips to help me with my poor shooting. He said "First, select the most perfectly round stones. The more perfectly round the stones are, the more accurate they will be."

He showed me how to hold the slingshot, how to aim it and the proper release. Most importantly, he told me, "You can be the best shot on the island, all you have to is to put your mind to it, and say to yourself I can do this, I can do anything I want."

Grandfather further told me, "You have to do research on the sport, research that will enable you to know all you need to know about hunting, its safety, and its purpose." He also told me, *"Maintain a positive attitude, concentrate on what you are doing, and practice often.* If you follow these instructions, you will become a master with a slingshot." Grandfather specifically told me, *"If you apply these principles to whatever you do in life, you can master anything."*

Grandfather gave me some pamphlets on hunting, which I read. I also followed his instructions closely, and within two weeks I was hitting everything I aimed at with my slingshot.

On the next hunting trip, I asked my cousins if I could have the first shot. They both agreed, they knew I would miss. They also knew it would keep me quiet for the remainder of the trip.

When the first shot was available, there were two grouse a short distance apart from each other. It was agreed that my target would be the nearest to me, and my cousin Ricky would take a shot at the one further away.

I took aim and shot down my target; I quickly reloaded and almost downed the second grouse before Ricky took his shot. My cousins knew how difficult it was to down one bird, but getting off a second shot was very difficult. My cousins were very impressed and proud of my accomplishments.

Aside from hunting grouse, another one of my favorite pastimes was rocking on a hammock. Our hammock was tied to two supporting posts underneath the house. As I swung on it, I would listen to the radio. I enjoyed the cool breeze on my face, as I listened to my favorite tune - "El Redecario."

I would use the hammock after my chores had been completed, or just to enjoy myself. My chores were to fetch water when needed from the common water pump located fifty yards from our house, and to pick fresh fruit from the fruit trees.

We had lemon trees, orange trees, grapefruit trees, mango trees, avocado trees and banana plants. I also picked fresh vegetables from Grandma's garden. My other chore was to help my grandfather feed the animals.

During the heavy rains, fruit would fall from the nearby fruit trees, and would be washed down the trenches located on both sides of the street. My cousins and I would place our shirts across the trenches to catch the flowing fruit.

I had not seen my mother for several years. However, I would see my brother and sister at family reunions. I longed to be reunited with Mom, Manny and Lucy. I always dreamed of our family being together again, besides I missed my mother dearly.

At times I was not sure what she looked like, so I would stare at a family photograph hanging on the living room wall. I would stare at the photograph for long periods of time, and daydream. Now I would be seeing her soon, and I longed for her arrival.

I thought that my life, as I knew it, would all change. My grandfather told me that in the United States, people had water and bathrooms inside their houses, there were stores nearby, and plenty of children for me to play with.

When our mother arrived, I was very impressed when I saw her. She was more beautiful than I had remembered. I had also forgotten how kind and caring she was.

Mom would *always put other people first.* Relatives and friends would use her as a means to get accurate advice when needed. Mom had taken after her father when it came to helping others with their problems. She had her father's wisdom.

Mom would ask many questions prior to giving out any advice. When she did, she would often end by telling them, *"Make sure that no one gets hurt by the decisions you make, and to try to keep other people's feelings, and their dignity in mind." She would especially stress that, "A person's dignity is something no one should take away."*

Mom told me that we would be leaving for the states within several months. Meanwhile, she had to take care of some family business. She had to sell our house, and visit some relatives and some of her old friends. Mom did not want to leave and then have to return to take care of something she overlooked.

Grandfather told me that the United States government had issued a check to my mother, and that my father had two life insurance policies, one he personally obtained when he entered the military, and the other was a family life insurance policy.

Mother told me when we return to America, she would use the money to purchase a home for the family. Mom stayed with us at her parent's house, and we would visit Lucy and Manny as often as possible. On these trips I would accompany her, and she would tell me how nice America was. She would also teach me English during our journey.

I was excited, because I heard many wonderful things about America. I also wondered if America was as beautiful as Puerto Rico, "The Beautiful Island" I would be leaving.

The news that I would be relocating to America traveled very quickly. Most of my friends knew about it in the neighborhood, and also at my school. One day after school, a schoolmate whom I didn't know well, walked up to me, punched me very hard, then ran away. I had no idea why he did such a thing.

That evening I told Grandfather about the incident, and asked him, "Why would he do such a thing to me. I hardly know him." Grandfather told me, "Going to America was a wonderful thing, and some of my schoolmates might be a bit envious."

I told Grandfather that tomorrow I was going to get even with the boy who had hit me. Grandfather told me that hitting that boy back was not going to solve anything, except create more attention and additional problems.

Grandfather also mentioned that, "Aggressive behavior should only be used as a last resort, and only when necessary."

My reply was that many of my friends had witnessed the incident and were expecting me to retaliate. Grandfather told me that, *"One should not allow peer pressure to control one's life. One has to be a leader and learn to control situations as well as their own life."*

The next day, after school, I approached the boy who had hit me. I grabbed the boy's collar, pulled him toward me, and told him that what he did yesterday was wrong, and that if he ever hit me again I was going to break his nose. The boy apologized to me in front of many of my friends.

After the incident, I realized that Grandfather was right. *There are many ways to take care of problems without resorting to violence.* I was very proud of how I had handled the entire matter, and that evening I told Grandfather a detailed account of the incident.

Grandfather responded by telling me, *"Those who live a good life will receive good things in return, and they will make friends and be respected by others."*

Finally, the day I dreamed about was here. I had my bags packed and said goodbye to my grandparents and my cousins. I was happy, yet apprehensive. I was going to a new country I knew little about. How would I communicate? The only English I spoke was the little I had learned at school, and what Mom had taught me.

Chapter Two

"The Concrete Island"

My first airplane ride was a memorable experience. I sat by a window so I could see the beautiful island I was leaving. I also thought that I would be the first of my siblings to see New York.

I was going to America, that wonderful world everyone talked about at my school. However, all I could see from my seat was the right wing of the plane and the two propellers attached to it.

Somewhere mid-way through our journey, I watched the inner propeller turning quickly. Suddenly it stopped turning. I became petrified and thought that I would never see America. I told Mom what I had observed. Seconds later the captain announced that the propeller had stopped, but that it would not interfere with the flight.

I was still afraid, and asked myself, "What if another propeller were to stop?" Fortunately, the pilot was able to restart the motor, and the propeller was once again making that loud roaring sound. This put my fears at rest.

My big concern during my journey was my grandfather. I would miss him dearly. My grandfather was a very good and kind gentleman. He was always there for me. He was also my best friend.

Most importantly he would give me advice when I needed it. Who would I turn to now? I knew my mother was just like Grandfather. She too would help and advise others, but she was a woman; and besides, I had a great relationship with my grandfather.

My only consolation was the parting words my grandfather told me when we said goodbye; he said, "If you need anything just write to me, I'll be there for you."

The airplane landed in an airport located in New Jersey called Teterboro. We were picked up by Anna, Mom's cousin, and taken to the Chelsea section of New York. While in route, I heard my first big band tune, Glenn Miller's "In the Mood."

I was amazed at everything I saw, all the roads were paved, the trees had very few leaves on them, and the ones that had leaves had beautiful colors; some were brown, some yellow, red, and many others beautiful colors.

The weather was also much colder. I had forgotten that New York had four different seasons. With much enthusiasm I could not wait to see my first snowfall.

Everywhere I looked I saw automobiles. At home I would only see them when we visited the larger cities.

We arrived in New York City, and every eyeful was another experience. To enter the city we drove through a tunnel. Anna told us it was the Lincoln Tunnel, and went underneath the Hudson River.

My brother and sister were also amazed, because they just looked with wide opened eyes at the new and incredible sites. We saw high-rise buildings, taxi cabs, and many people. I had learned at school that Manhattan was an island; as we drove on, I thought to myself, "It's a concrete island."

Our new living quarters were located in the Chelsea section of Manhattan. It was a small three bedroom apartment located on the second floor of a seven story building. One bedroom was for Mom, one for Lucy, and the third bedroom would be shared by my brother and me.

Our apartment was called a cold water flat. This meant it had cold running water and no heat. To heat the apartment we used several kerosene stoves.

The apartment had an ice box to store our perishables. An ice man would deliver the block ice that was placed inside a small compartment in the ice box to keep things cold. During the winter season, Mom would use a window box located on the window ledge to keep things cold.

The best thing I liked was the common bathroom located in the hallway of every floor. Behind the toilet there was a water tank attached to the wall several feet above the toilet. It had a pull chain, which was used to flush the toilet.

The far end of the toilet contained a shower with cold and hot running water. I would no longer walk twenty feet in the dark evenings to use the outhouse, as I was accustomed to at my grandmother and grandfather's house. Also impressive was the small sink located in our kitchen with running cold water.

Lucy and I were enrolled in PS 33, a local Manhattan elementary school located on 9th Avenue. Manny was enrolled in the local high school. Lucy and I adapted very well. We made many friends and were rapidly learning the English language.

We were placed in lower grades than most children our age, only because of our poor language abilities. There were no English language courses available for students who were from other countries. Non-English speakers had to learn English on their own.

Manny, on the other hand was very discontent and rebellious. He missed his homeland, his friends, and a female acquaintance for whom he had developed an interest. Manny was also opposed to learning the English language.

He had also developed a negative attitude toward school, people, and numerous other things. Due to his negative attitude, he was involved in many fights.

To make matters worse, his peers were at the age in which bigotry was prevalent. Manny quickly learned what the English word Spic meant. Instead of ignoring the name calling, he would use his fists to retaliate.

Manny fought so often that it began to affect his grades. He also developed the reputation of being a bully. He was involved in so many fights that he became good at it. He learned to punch first and punch hard. He became one of the toughest kids in the school.

Because of this reputation, he was invited to join the "Los Ojos," which means the eyes, a Hispanic gang which kept a watchful eye on other

Hispanics in the neighborhood. The gang members of the "Los Ojos" wore blue jackets, with two eyes on the back. Their gang leaders wore red jackets to identify their status.

In a nearby neighborhood there was another Hispanic gang - "Los Lobos" - who would on occasion have turf battles with the "Los Ojos." These turf battles began several years before, when the "Los Lobos" were asked to assist another Hispanic gang from the Bronx, the "Los Latinos," in their turf battle.

The leader of the "Los Lobos" asked the leader of the "Los Ojos" to join them in helping the "Los Latinos." The leader of the "Los Ojos" refused to help. Their reply was, "We will help you to fight against the white gangs or the black gangs in our own neighborhood, but we would not go fight out of our area." Since then, the two gangs began to distance themselves. Their views and interests became different, and turf battles between the two began.

Membership in the "Los Ojos" caused Manny to stay out late at night, and he developed many changes in his behavior and his personality. He began to smoke, curse, and most importantly, lose his self-respect.

I wasn't sure, but I had a gut feeling that Manny's gang may have been involved in some illegal activities. My feelings were based on the large amounts of money Manny would have, and the expensive clothes and jewelry he would wear.

Manny continued with his fighting. He would fight anyone at any time. He had no fear, nor any respect for others. Manny didn't use many words in confrontations, just fists. Because of his fighting, he was suspended many times from school.

Mother would often be summoned to school for Manny's fighting, poor attitude and unacceptable behavior. On many occasions, Lucy and I would overhear Mom as she tried to talk to Manny. She blamed herself, and we would hear her crying in her bed at night.

Mom began to question herself, by asking herself, "Did I make the right decision of exposing my family to this environment?" However, because she was a resourceful woman, she came up with an idea. She would relocate her family to New Jersey. Houses were also cheaper in New Jersey.

One night, just before bedtime, Manny was tending to his bleeding nose. He had been in a fight earlier and had been punched in the nose. I asked him why he fought so often. He told me it was a matter of survival; besides, he had to uphold his respect and reputation.

I asked him what he got out of fighting. Manny responded, "It is the way of the street". I told him, "Someday you might meet someone who is stronger and tougher than you. Then someone is going to get seriously hurt."

I also told Manny, "I don't fight unless it is absolutely necessary, and I have many friends, a good reputation and I think I am well-respected."

Manny responded by asking me, "What do you do when someone calls you names?" I responded that my friends and I have a saying, *"Sticks and stones may break my bones, but names will never hurt me."* I truly believe this.

One summer evening, while I was playing at the nearby playground, I overheard a conversation between Papo and Manny. Manny, because of his toughness and aggressive behavior, had moved up to the top rank in the "Los Ojos." Papo was second in command.

The conversation revealed that on Saturday night there would be a confrontation with the "Los Lobos." Manny told Papo, "We have to put the "Los Lobos" completely out of business. This has to be it. This must be the final battle, and it could only happen if we really hurt them."

I did not know what to do, but I knew that someone had to stop this gang war between the two gangs. I had remembered the advice my grandfather had once given to me, *"Nothing is ever resolved by fighting, it only creates more problems and pain."*

I also loved my brother and didn't want anything to happen to him. I then remembered my grandfather's parting words, "If you ever need anything write to me I will be there for you." I knew I could not turn to my grandfather, only because the mail system would be too slow, and the fight was three days away. What could I to do?

My walk home only brought me more concern when my eyes caught sight of a beggar with no legs and one stubby arm. He would use his good arm to wheel his body around on a wooden board, which was mounted on roller skate wheels.

I had seen many men like him on the streets. Most of them were veterans who had been wounded. My first thought was of my father. Then I thought of my brother, who could wind up seriously hurt and maybe even paralyzed.

I wanted to talk Manny out of going to the gang war on Saturday evening, but I couldn't. My reason was if I were to tell him the conversation I had overheard, Manny would accuse me of snooping. Furthermore, I didn't want to lose the trust we had between us.

If I were to tell our mother, I was sure an argument would ensue between her and Manny. This would only worsen their relationship.

Involving Mom would also worry her, and she had enough to worry about. I was also concerned that by telling Mom, Manny would accuse me of squealing.

I would talk to Lucy. I will tell Lucy what I had overheard, and ask her to talk to Manny. I would also tell Lucy not to tell Manny where she had obtained the information. Lucy was my only hope. Besides, I believed Lucy was the person who might be able to talk some sense into Manny. Manny loved her and would always look after his younger sister.

I spoke to Lucy, and told her of the meeting between Manny and Papo, and what I had overheard. I told her she had to try and stop the fight, and I asked her not to reveal to Manny where she had obtained the information.

I also told Lucy I believed Manny respected her good judgment. Lucy agreed. Lucy told me she had heard from her friends that the "Los Lobos" were out to get Manny. Lucy spoke to Manny, and begged him not to go. Manny told Lucy that his men were depending on him, and that he would not let his men down. Manny also told her, "If I don't show up for the fight, I would be called a coward; besides I like a good fight."

Lucy told me of the conversation she had with Manny, and how Manny would be attending the turf battle. Lucy also told me that our mother was now the only solution.

Lucy and I told Mother of the big fight which was to take place on Saturday night. When Manny came home, Mom told him she had heard about the fight on Saturday. She told him she did not want him to attend. She further talked about how fighting was childish and senseless.

Manny responded that he had to go, "It's a matter of respect from my peers." Mom told him, "This is the type of respect that you don't need and shouldn't want. Do you think I brought you here and toil every day just so that you could be respected by a bunch of hoodlums?"

Mom stated, "I have lost your Father in a battle and I don't want to lose a son." Manny responded, "No one is going to get killed." Mother told him, *"Very often gang wars get out of control, and end up with someone getting hurt."* The argument got so out of control that Manny walked out of the apartment. Mother went into her room weeping.

I ran after my brother and told him that it was me who told Mom of the fight. I no longer cared if my brother knew where the information came from. The important thing was his safety.

I also told Manny I had overheard the conversation between him and Papo, and how I told Lucy and we both told Mom. The reason we told her was because we loved him and didn't want anything to happen to him. Manny told me that he loved us too, and asked me to return home.

I left Manny and headed home. Manny walked the street in a confused state. He loved his family, but he had a reputation to uphold. He had to choose, would he choose his family, or would he be the hero his gang members believed him to be?

Saturday night came and sometime after dinner Manny told Mother he was not going out. He walked into his bedroom, shut the door, and snuck out through the fire escape. He would often use this sneak out technique when he went out late at night.

I was very much aware of Manny's trick. I waited for a moment, and proceeded to follow him.

Manny walked toward the rendezvous location. As he walked, he thought about what Mother had said about losing our father and how she didn't want to lose a son.

He also thought about what I had told him, how Lucy and I loved him. Manny was getting second thoughts about going, but what excuse would he use. He would have to give them a very convincing reason - after all he was their leader.

He was well aware of the consequences. He would be an outcast and be called a coward. Not only would he lose his rank within the gang, he would be ousted. He had a reputation to uphold. He made up his mind, he would attend the fight.

I called Manny's name. Manny heard me calling him, but did not respond. I then yelled to him, "If you are going to fight and get hurt, so am I." Manny yelled back, "That is out of the question, you are too young." Manny did not want me to get hurt, so he ran as fast as he could in an effort to lose me.

I darted across the street as I kept a close watch on my brother. Out of nowhere a car appeared; the driver applied his brakes but was unable to stop in time. The car hit me, throwing me onto the sidewalk.

Manny heard the screeching of the tires and the thumping sound. He headed back and found me lying on the sidewalk. I was taken to the hospital via an ambulance and Manny rode with me. I was examined, and my only injury was a broken arm. I could not obtain any medical attention until Mom arrived, because her permission was required.

The wait seemed forever, and I was petrified. My fear brought me a very deep and serious sob. I was scared as I thought of the man on the street with his stubby arm. My thought was of losing my arm. I asked myself, "At what juncture would the doctors cut off my arm?"

I had broken it about three inches from the wrist. Will they cut off my arm at the broken point or at the elbow? Manny waited with me; he could not sign the permission slip for the hospital to treat me, because he was just short of his eighteenth birthday.

Finally, I asked my brother where he thought the doctors would cut off my arm. Manny told me they were not going to cut off my arm. The doctors were going to reset it. Everything was going to be all right, and my arm would be as good as new.

Manny then realized the anguish I was going through. To think the doctors were going to cut off my arm. He also realized how much he loved me, and told me so.

He also told me that from now on he was going to take care of me as our father would have. Manny thought to himself, "I have just told my brother that I was going to take care of him, but in reality my younger brother had just taken care of me. He has given me the best excuse for not attending the gang war."

Mother arrived, signed the necessary papers and I was brought to surgery. Mom, Manny and Lucy stayed at the hospital until early in the morning.

When I woke up I had a cast on my left arm, from the middle of my bicep to my finger joints. I saw my fingers and was able to move them. I felt a throbbing pain, but I was very happy because the doctor did not cut off any part of my arm.

The doctor told me I would have to wear the cast for six to eight weeks, and afterwards I would have to do exercises to regain movement. I would have to slowly move my elbow and wrist until I got full mobility.

I stayed in the hospital for three days. Afterwards, I was released and able to go back to school.

Manny's mind was made up to leave the gang. His plan was to gradually wean himself from the gang. He would appoint Papo as their new leader, and Jose to be second in command. Manny knew that Papo and Jose had a good relationship. Therefore, no objections would be made to the appointments.

The next day Manny found out from a friend, not a gang member, that Papo had been stabbed, and was in the hospital in critical condition. Manny also found out that the police had made many arrests.

The word on the street was that the judge would not tolerate any more gang violence, and there was a rumor that the judge was going to impose heavy sentences on both the adults and the juveniles involved in the fracas.

Manny went to the gang hangout; as he entered the sleazy store, he felt the thickness of the air. One gang member looked down on Manny as he passed. Another spit on the floor, and the rest would not acknowledge Manny's presence.

Finally, one asked where he had been last night. He responded his younger brother had broken his arm, and he had taken him to the hospital.

They did not believe him and called him a coward and a yellow belly. They did so only because they knew they had him outnumbered. They would not dare challenge him on a one-to-one, or in fact on a two-to-one basis. For now, the odds were in their favor and they believed they had the upper hand.

Manny finally realized that no matter what he said, they would not believe him. One gang member pointed at Manny and stated, "You were the Lobos' real target, and you should be the one dying at the hospital, not Papo." Manny took off his gang jacket, threw it on the floor and stated, "You can all shove your jacket and your gang."

Manny left the store and walked the streets thinking how he had wasted his last several years with a bunch of worthless hoods, and worst of all he was one of them. He had to somehow change his life. His mother, his brother, and his sister were right. He thought how he had to change. He would start by controlling his temper, try to do better in school, and get a job.

Manny walked home and as soon as he arrived, he told his family that he had left the gang, and that he was going to change. He told them of his plans. Mother told us, *"We are very fortunate because we have each other, and that no matter what happens in the future, we should all know we can confide and depend on each other."*

Mom continued, *"Any future problems should be shared with the family. We have to talk with each other and know we have each other for support. We have to be strong and endure when we are tempted, and going through trials. We must learn from our mistakes, reflect on them, and move on."*

The next evening during dinner, Manny told us, "It was my little brother who had gotten me out of a very serious situation." Manny said, "It was me who the "Los Lobos" gang was after, and it could have been me in the hospital with the stab wound." Manny thanked and hugged me. I told them, "My brother is worth much more than a broken arm."

Manny did change, his grades improved, he was able to control his temper, and obtained a job working at a nearby grocery store. He would perform all duties, such as stock shelves, operate the cash register, clean, wait on customers and even do the inventory.

On one occasion, the store was held up by two young men. One had a small caliber revolver, and the other a hunting knife. Manny, who was in the back room, overheard the conversation. He quietly telephoned the police, and snuck up behind the two men with a baseball bat.

He hit the man with the gun on the arm which held the weapon. The weapon flew across the store, and landed under the soup shelves. His accomplice immediately ran out the door. Manny wrestled with the suspect and was able to hold him until the police arrived. The police called them the soup bandits, because there were soup cans everywhere.

Manny received a hero's award from the New York City Police Department. He also received a letter from the Major. Manny was very proud of what he had done, he felt good about himself for the first time in his life. This incident was a major turning point in his life.

Manny was contacted by Jose, who was now the head of the "Los Ojos" gang. Gang members found out that Manny's little brother had in fact been hit by a car and taken to the hospital by Manny on the evening of the gang war.

They now believed Manny's story and wanted him to return to the gang as their head. Jose also told Manny that Papo had recovered, and the person who stabbed him was apprehended and was presently in jail. Manny refused Jose's offer.

One day Manny asked me, "For such a young person, where did you get all of your wisdom from?" I told him, "I had received it from living with Grandpa. He would always talk to me, and give me good advice on important matters."

I also told him, "I have kept all of my grandfather's letters, letters which contain many old sayings and Grandpa's words of wisdom." Manny's response was, "Lucy and I were not as fortunate."

I would write often to my grandfather and keep him updated on family matters. I would not hide anything from him. I would provide him with specific details on all events. Grandfather would write me back and continue to guide me as he had always done, always inspiring me.

My grandfather, in his own way, was trying to bring out the best in me. I believed he wanted me to be a good and successful person. He wanted me to be like him, a gentle and kind man, a man everyone looked up to.

Several months later Mother broke the good news to the family. She told us that we were going to move to New Jersey. She had seen and put down a deposit on a two and a half family house in Paterson, New Jersey, and the bank had approved the loan. Three weeks later Mom hired a moving company, and we were in route to our new home.

CHAPTER THREE

"Love at First Sight"

We moved to our new house, a two and a half family house located on Park Avenue in the Eastside section of Paterson, New Jersey. The house was an older one but was in excellent shape. Our apartment was on the second floor, and had four bedrooms, so everyone had their own bedroom.

Manny's room was located near the front of the house and had a private entrance, which led to the front hallway. Therefore, he could come and go as he pleased. Mom had given Manny this bedroom only because he had regained her trust. He had become more mature and responsible in his decision making.

The house had two front porches, one as you entered the house, and the other on the second floor. It was a perfect location to watch the parades that would start at City Hall and march to Eastside Park.

The parades would travel down Park Avenue and pass in front of our house. There would be many vendors on both sides of the streets, who sold food, drinks, toys, flags and my favorite - salty pretzels.

The house had both hot and cold running water. It had a bathroom with both a bath tub and a sink. The house was also heated by a coal furnace. It was my job to feed the coal into the furnace and bank it at night. I also would shovel the used ashes from the bottom of the furnace and put them into metal pails. The same pails I would put out during garbage collection days.

Coal would be delivered to our house on a monthly winter schedule. If we ran short, Mom would call Slater Coal Company, and a delivery would be made on the following day. The coal truck would back onto the sidewalk and a coal chute was placed from the truck into a window leading into a coal bin located in our cellar. The delivery man would then shovel coal onto the chute, which slid into the coal bin.

Two things I liked about our new house were that it had push button switches to turn the lights on and off, and most importantly, a telephone.

On the first floor lived the Henderson family, who had a daughter April and a son Edward. Both children were several years younger than me. The third floor apartment was a small apartment, which had just been renovated and was currently unoccupied.

The nearest Catholic church was Saint Joseph's located on the corners of Market and Carroll Streets. Our family enrolled at St. Joseph's, and immediately Monsignor Shanley placed me in the Confirmation Program.

I was confirmed the following May, and for my confirmation Mom had a nice confirmation party. Family members and many friends attended. Mom gave me my first rosary beads, which were blessed by Bishop McNulty.

Manny and Lucy were enrolled at Eastside High School, and I began my last year at Public School Number 15. School number 15 was located on Sandy Hill, and was at one end of Sandy Hill Park.

I was a good student, and was always striving to improve. My grandfather would keep after me, and would often ask me in his letters how I was doing in school. My grandfather always stressed the importance of an education. He told me in one of his letters, *"An education is the avenue to success and the foundation to achieving one's goals."*

The school year passed quickly, and before long I had graduated PS 15. I began my first year at Eastside H.S. It was on my first day of school when it happened. As I entered into my Ancient History class, there she was, the most beautiful girl in the world.

I couldn't take my eyes off her, and when she looked at me I would get chills all over my body. It was love at first sight.

I sat next to her, but I knew if I were to sit in this seat all semester I would have surely failed. Fortunately, the teacher sat the students in alphabetical order. In my new assigned seat, this beautiful person sat two rows away from and behind me. If I turned around to stare at her, it would become obvious to the other students that I was interested in her.

My heart would pound so hard when she was near me that I could hear it throbbing. She was slender, tall, had a light complexion, a good figure, dark blue eyes, and wavy dark brown hair.

I knew for the first time in my life I was in love, and wanted to be with her for the rest of my life. I had never felt like this before, nor was I interested in girls before, but she was special.

Ancient History was the last class for the day. After class I walked out with Jay Pearlman. Jay had blond hair, green eyes, stocky build, and had graduated from PS 15 with me. He lived in one of the biggest houses in the Eastside Park area of Paterson.

Jay was considered a close friend. I asked him if he knew this beautiful girl called Stephanie Mullen. Jay replied he did not know her, but agreed she was beautiful. I told Jay that I was going to ask her to go out with me.

Jay laughed at me. I asked him why he was laughing, and he replied, "Tony, you have a very slim chance of going out with her, she is out of our class, and especially you being a Puerto Rican."

My response was, "Do you think you as a Jew have a better chance?" Jay laughed and said, "That depends if she is Jewish." My answer was, "With a last name like Mullen, I doubt she is Jewish."

I told Jay my grandfather had once told me, *"If you want something bad enough, no matter what it may be, you have to go after it. If you don't try you will never succeed, nor will you ever know if you could have obtained it. It is better to try and fail than not try at all."* I told Jay, "Just you wait and see what happens."

That evening at the dinner table I told my family about Stephanie. I asked them for advice on how to approach her, what to say to her, and what girls liked?

Lucy began by telling me the topics I should talk to her about, and what girls liked about boys. Mom told me that girls like boys who are gentle, kind, and treat them with respect.

Manny was quiet, but later in the evening, he visited me in my bedroom. Manny talked to me about the birds and the bees, expounding on what Mom had mentioned about respect.

I wrote to Grandfather and told him about Stephanie, and how I felt about her. I told him how my heart would patter when I was near her, or even when I just thought about her.

Several days later, I received a letter from Grandfather. In his letter he wrote, *"We all have dreams, and our job is to try to make our dreams come true."* Grandfather also gave me advice on how to approach her, how to behave, how to treat her, and a very long litany about the birds and the bees.

The first week of school passed very quickly and I spoke to Stephanie on only one occasion. On this day I managed to walk slowly down the hallway, until she caught up to me. I said hello to her and introduced myself. She replied, "I know who you are." When I asked how she knew my name, she stated, "I am in your history class!" I felt stupid and walked down the nearest stairway. Then I smiled as I thought, "She knows my name."

I was moving much slower than I wanted. I wanted to speed up my advances before any of the other boys. I had heard that some of the boys thought she was out of their league, so they were afraid of trying to date her.

I would try again on Monday, but this time I would be prepared. I went home and rehearsed all weekend in front of the mirror some of the questions I would ask her.

Monday after class, I again walked slowly until Stephanie caught up to me. I looked at her face and gazed into her beautiful blue eyes. Something happened to me because all I had rehearsed was forgotten. All I could say was what was on my mind; I told her, "I think you are beautiful." Stephanie thanked me, as I slipped down the nearest exit.

Again I blew it. What was I thinking? I blew it. I really wanted to ask her where she lived, and if I could walk her home.

At dinner table I told my family of my blunders. Lucy and Manny graciously continue to encourage me. Mom did mention that some girls at this age may not be ready to start dating, and that *there are many fish in the sea*. I knew that Mom was preparing me for a possible disappointment.

I tried to find out more information about her so I would be better prepared on our next meeting, but no one seemed to know her.

The third week of school was a disaster week. Stephanie was not in class all week. I thought perhaps she was ill, or maybe she moved. My heart was in my throat all week.

The next week came and went and no Stephanie. At the dinner table I would often talk about her, but after her disappearance I would just think about her and try not to mention her name. Was I subconsciously trying to forget her?

Stephanie was a no-show for the next three weeks of school, and I was really upset. My grandfather, whom I had updated about her disappearance, kept encouraging me to be positive.

On Sundays the family would attend the ten o'clock Sunday services at St. Joseph's Church. However, from this Sunday on we would be attending the nine o'clock services because Lucy and I had to go to CCD (Confraternity of Christian Doctrine) classes.

There were many children of all ages attending this Mass because it was mandatory that all students from St. Joseph's Elementary School and St. Joseph's High School, as well as any public school students enrolled in the religious instruction classes attend..

I was looking where the other high school students were seated to see if any of my friends were here. All of a sudden my eyes opened up very wide. There she was - it was Stephanie. She must have changed schools because she was sitting with the St. Joseph's High School students.

My heart began to palpitate. I felt that same feeling I had when I first met her. I pointed Stephanie out to Mom, who was seated next to me. Mom's reply was that she was more beautiful than she had imagined.

Mom passed the word on, and before long the whole family was in on it, they all wanted to get a better look at her.

I knew I had to make my move after Mass, and before my religious instructions. I did not want her to get away again.

After Mass I walked up to her, said hello, and told her that I had missed her being in class. She replied that that was a sweet of me to say that. She told me she had transferred to St. Joseph's School.

I asked her where she lived and she replied that she lived near Eastside Park. I really wanted to know her exact address so I could visit her.

Stephanie then asked me if I was going to the CYO (Catholic Youth Organization) Dance tomorrow night. I asked her where the dance was being held. She replied it was at her school at 7:00 PM. I asked her if she was going and she stated, "Yes." I told her I would meet her there.

An adult couple walked up to us, it appeared they could be her parents. I quickly told Stephanie I had to leave because I had to attend CCD class.

All through CCD Class I was on cloud nine. I wasn't sure, but I believed she had asked me for a date. I was a bit apprehensive about going to the dance. The simple reason was I did not know how to dance.

That Sunday evening, Lucy and Manny gave me two hours of dance lessons. I was not a great dancer, but I was told I was gentle and smooth - not bad for a beginner.

Monday, during Ancient History class, I asked Jay if he wanted to go to the C.Y.O. dance with me. Jay asked me what C.Y.O. meant, and after I told him he said, "I can't go – I am Jewish." I told him he could be my guest. He then asked me if there would be any services there. I told him it was just a dance. He agreed to go. I think the real reason he wanted to go was to see if I really had a date with Stephanie.

Jay and I met with Stephanie at the dance. She was with one of her classmates, a girl named Ann Sheldon. Stephanie introduced Ann to Jay and me. Jay danced with Ann, and they hit it off well. Stephanie and I could see they were meant for each other. However, if their relationship were to get serious, they and their families would have to face this interfaith (Catholic/Jewish) relationship.

At the dance, I danced most of the slow dances with Stephanie. While we danced I felt chills and a warm sensation throughout my entire body. I wanted to squeeze her with all my might, but I remembered my grandfather's letters, which told me that *girls are fragile and one should treat them with gentleness.*

We conversed with each other, and I found out she was several months younger, was the only child, and lived on Manor Drive near Eastside Park. We asked each other many questions to get better acquainted, and finally we exchanged telephone numbers.

After the last dance I waited outside with her until her mother arrived to pick her up. Jay and I walked home and talked about the girls and how much fun we had.

Stephanie and I would often talk on the telephone. On occasions I would meet her during weekdays and take long walks through Eastside Park. As we walked we would hold hands, and I would once again feel that warm sensation throughout my entire body.

Monday evenings were considered our date night, and would see each other at the CYO Dances. Jay and Ann would also attend. On one Monday evening, Jay and I went to the men's room. Inside there were three boys singing a cappella. They sounded very good. One of the boys asked Jay and I if we wanted to sing with them.

We sang a few songs with them, and became part of their group. We would meet every Monday during CYO and take a few minutes to sing a few songs. We would also meet on other occasions in a home or on the street corner just to sing. Jay and I made a promise not to tell Ann or Stephanie about our group until we were sure we would not embarrass ourselves.

Stephanie and I would also meet at basketball games, football games, and during the spring season at baseball games.

We fell in love with each other and became very good friends. We did as my grandfather had told me in his letters – *have a lot of fun and make each other happy.*

I believed Stephanie's mother, Mary, liked me. She was tall, slender, well-built, had brown hair, and blue eyes. She was kind, gentle and intelligent. She looked like Stephanie, but Stephanie was more beautiful.

Stephanie's father, Robert, was a tall man, had light brown hair, blue eyes, medium build, and was one of the big wigs at the Morning Call News newspaper. He was also in the process of starting a company, which would build parts for government aircraft.

I had a feeling Stephanie's father did not like me, and he was allowing time to separate us. His feeling was that this romance was just a high school thing and would blow away in time. My gut feeling was he believed nobody was good enough for his little girl.

Due to his busy schedule, Stephanie's father had seen me on just a few occasions. One day he asked his wife if she knew my last name. She told him it was Herera. All at once he blurted out, "He's a Puerto Rican boy, why didn't you tell me this?" His wife responded, "Does it matter? He is a very nice boy. He is intelligent, he is doing well in school, and Stephanie likes him. They also get along very well, and they have a lot of fun together."

Stephanie's father was angry and told his wife he was under the impression that I was an Italian boy. Now that he knows what I am he has to do something about it. He has to break up this relationship as soon as possible.

Mrs. Mullen warned him not to do that, "If you break them up, you would be hurting Stephanie, and she could possibly end up hating you."

Stephanie's father made an agreement with his wife that he would not interfere in their relationship. However, in his mind he was giving this relationship until they graduated from high school. If they were still together at that time, he would do all in his power to break it up. He wanted only the best for his daughter, and I was not a part of his plan.

During my junior year I obtained my driver's license. Manny had taught me how to drive and was very generous with letting me borrow his car. Driving brought Stephanie and me more freedom, and gave us more time to be together.

Stephanie and I had been so busy attending school functions, games, and dances, that we never had a chance to be alone for extensive periods of time. With a car available, we were able to go to the Totowa Drive-In Theater, where we could talk and make out.

On one such occasion, it came to the point where the urge to have sex was more than we could stand. *At this point Stephanie told me that she loved me, and because she loved me she was saving herself for me. She meant on our wedding night.*

I tried with all my might to get Stephanie to change her mind. I even told her that the boys in my classes are all doing it. Stephanie responded, "You are not one of those boys, and I am not one of those girls."

I then made a big mistake and told her that there were other girls. Stephanie came on very strong and said to me, "If you really love me, and respect me you wouldn't do that." She also told me, "I am saving myself just for you, and you should save yourself just for me." With a very stern and sincere voice she said, *"If you want to do that with another girl, then we could end our relationship right now."*

This was our first fight. I apologized and told her I didn't want anyone else. I assured her she was the only one for me, and I didn't want to lose her.

When things cooled down, I told her that my grandfather had written to me when I had first met her, and basically told me the same thing she had just mentioned in one of his letters.

Stephanie told me, "Then you should know better." She also told me she liked the way my grandfather thinks, and that I should be more like him.

I asked her where she had gotten her information, and she told me from her mother and from her teacher Sister Maggie, who taught sex education at St. Joe's School.

There were no winners in this fight. We both knew where each other stood and we established commonalities, such as our feelings, mutual respect and expectations of each other.

Stephanie and I continued to date, and every day our relationship grew stronger and stronger. We got to know each other very well and were happy with the way the other responded to life, life's pleasures and life's hardships. Not only did we love each other, but we were very good friends.

Stephanie's mother grew more attached to me. She trusted and respected me. Her father was still waiting for our break up. He was hoping it would come as a natural thing. He was hoping perhaps at college Stephanie would meet another young man, an American boy.

My family was doing well. Mom was working in an Italian restaurant for several years. She had money left over from Dad's life insurance, and was receiving rent from the first floor and from the third floor apartments, which had been rented to a widow.

Lucy had graduated Eastside High and was working as a secretary for a dye house in the Riverside section of Paterson. She was also dating John Moore, a senior at Seton Hall University.

John was a true Irishman; he had a light complexion, was tall, with blue eyes, dark brown hair, and a medium build. John was majoring in education, and had intentions of becoming a high school math teacher.

John and I got along very well, and John would on occasion help me with my math homework. John also had a domineering mother, who would keep a tight leash on John's life.

Manny had also graduated Eastside High School, and was working for the Allied Trucking Company as a truck driver. He would travel short routes within New Jersey. On occasion, he would take longer routes and would be away for several days. During his long trips I would look after his car.

Manny was dating a Puerto Rican girl name Gladys Mendez. Gladys was pretty, had dark brown hair, dark brown eyes, and was well-built, with a fair complexion. Gladys worked at Meyer Brothers Department Store as a cashier. They had been dating for two years and were a great couple.

We lived on Park Avenue for several years, and Mom had intentions of buying a one family house in another section of Paterson. Mom's intention was to keep our current house for income. This added income would help pay for my upcoming college tuition.

My junior year at Eastside, I received my graduation ring, and tradition was to attend the Ring Cotillion Dinner/Dance. The dinner was held at the Alexander Hamilton Hotel. Stephanie and I double-dated with Jay and Ann, who were still dating. At the dance I gave Stephanie my graduation ring to wear as a symbol of going together. Jay also gave his ring to Ann.

During the latter part of my junior year, a telephone call from Puerto Rico advised us that Mom's mother had passed away. Grandfather was able to use a neighbor's telephone to contact us. Telephone calls from Puerto Rico came during emergencies, and this call allowed the members of our family in the U.S. an opportunity to attend the funeral services in P.R.

Manny and I would not be able to attend. I was in the middle of final examinations, and Manny would be away on a road trip for his company. Therefore, Mom, Lucy and Mom's cousin were the only ones who would be able to make the funeral services.

They stayed in Puerto Rico for two weeks, and upon their return, they brought back my grandfather. Mom thought it would be better if her father were to visit us in New Jersey, to help him get over his wife's death and get a chance to see his favorite grandchildren, whom he loved dearly.

I did not know Grandfather was coming, and I was surprised and elated when I arrived at Newark Airport to pick them up and saw Grandfather with them.

I introduced Stephanie to Grandfather, and they immediately became attached to each other. They felt they knew and understood each other.

Stephanie and I spent much time with my grandfather. We introduced him to people, showed him the city of Paterson, took him to see wrestling matches at the Paterson Armory, and we even took him to see the Yankees play. The Yankees were always Grandfather's favorite team.

I had to serve as an interpreter for Grandfather, who was a first time visitor to America and spoke little English.

Grandfather told me he liked Stephanie, and sensed that she was very much in love with me. He also told me to treat her well, because she will make an excellent wife. My response was, "I know she loves me, and I love her very much." I also told him, "I treat her like a princess."

Stephanie became acquainted with my grandfather, and told me she was impressed with his kindness, gentleness, and wisdom. I told her to remind me to someday show her the letters my grandfather had written to me, letters which contain many phrases full of wonderful words of wisdom. I told her I had saved all of them, and would read them over and over. I would also refer to them whenever they became applicable to a situation in my life.

Grandfather stayed with us for the most of the summer, and would be returning to Puerto Rico in late August. Shortly before I went back to school, I found Grandfather sitting on our sofa. He had a heart attack and passed away while taking a short nap.

I was very sad. Once again I had lost another hero. On the other hand, I was happy that he died a peaceful death, a death becoming a gentleman.

The family, both in Puerto Rico and in the States, agreed that Grandfather should be buried in New Jersey. It would be a big expense to fly him to Puerto Rico. Furthermore, we believed that he, being buried in a cemetery next to his wife, is not important; the important belief is they would be reunited in heaven.

Family members, friends, and Stephanie and her family attended the funeral service, which was held at St. Joseph's Church. Interment was at Calvary Cemetery. Afterwards, the family went to our house for the repast.

Mom cooked her special Spanish dishes. The food was very tasty and was enjoyed by all. Mr. Mullen complemented Mom on her cooking, and Mrs. Mullen asked for some of Mom's recipes.

The end of summer was near, and one weekend Stephanie's family invited me to go sailing with them. The Mullens had a 36-foot sailing boat called "Stephanie," which they stored on the bay at a Seaside Heights marina.

On this trip, Mr. Mullen taught me the basics of sailing, and was overheard by Stephanie as he told Mrs. Mullen that I was a fast learner and would make a good sailor.

That day we sailed, swam, and had a very fine dinner at Captain Bill's Restaurant. Stephanie's mom felt her husband was finally starting to like me.

Stephanie's parents would invite me over for Sunday family picnics. They would have two or three picnics during the summer months. At these picnics, I would meet most of Stephanie's family. My favorite family members were Michael Mullen, Stephanie's father's cousin, his wife Sara, and their two well-behaved children, Johnny and Mary.

My job was to help Mr. Mullen cook. One time he asked me how my father had died. I told him he was shot while serving our country during World War II. He further asked me where he was buried. I told him in San German, Puerto Rico.

Stephanie and I enjoyed watching and playing with Johnny and Mary. Stephanie and I both loved children.

On one occasion, while Stephanie and I were eating, Mrs. Mullen told Sara, "Watch what Tony does with his chocolate chip cookie." I took one of Mrs. Mullen's great chocolate chip cookies, broke it in half and gave the other half to Stephanie.

Mrs. Mullen asked Sara, "Did you see what he did?" Sara said, "Yes, he gave her half his cookie." Mrs. Mullen then told Sara, "Did you notice he gave her the bigger half?"

My final year at Eastside High began, and I started to think about the colleges I wanted to attend. My first choice was Rutgers University. Stephanie wanted to attend a Catholic College in one of the southern states, but was not sure which one she would attend.

On weekends Stephanie and I would visit Grandfather's grave. On one visit, when I attended alone, I noticed three fresh cut red roses on the grave. Two of the roses were placed like the letter V, and the third was placed in the middle. The stems touched at the bottom.

I asked family members who had placed the flowers there, and no one knew. When I mentioned it to Stephanie, she told me she had visited Grandfather's grave, and had put the flowers there. Stephanie told me she liked my grandfather, the reason being that he reminded her of me.

CHAPTER FOUR

"Sometimes Life is Not Fair"

❊ Senior year at high school is supposed to be a great year, but not for me. One night, just after Thanksgiving, I heard Lucy crying in her bedroom. Through the closed door, I asked Lucy if she was all right. Lucy admitted me into her bedroom, closed the door, and told me she was going to have a baby.

Lucy told me she had found out that day. After work she had visited her doctor and he had told her the news. Lucy also indicated it was John's baby. She also stated several months ago they talked about getting married after John graduated college. However, that would be several months away.

I suggested they could get married earlier. Lucy agreed and responded she had the same idea, and was going to talk to John tomorrow. Lucy would tell him she was pregnant, and make arrangements for an earlier wedding. Afterwards, she would tell Mom.

I asked Lucy why she was crying, and Lucy responded she did not know how Mom would respond. I reminded Lucy that Mom, being a caring and gentle person, would understand. I also mentioned that knowing Mom, she would help Lucy with anything she needed. I assured Lucy that everything was going to be all right.

Lucy proceeded to lecture me on being careful so this same situation doesn't happen to Stephanie and me. I assured her it would not. I then reminded Lucy of a conversation we had just after I started dating Stephanie, a conversation in which Lucy told me *the importance of abstaining from sex until after one is married.* Lucy responded, "It was a weak moment for me, and sometimes it may take the other person to say no, *someone has to be strong.* Because John and I were both weak, we are now in this situation."

Lucy called John the next day from work, and asked John to meet her for dinner, John agreed and they made arrangements to meet at The Tree Tavern, located on Park Avenue. Lucy told John she had something to tell him, and John told her he had something to tell her.

After a quick welcoming kiss, they sat at a corner table. Lucy thought what John had to tell her was not as important as what she had to say, so she allowed John to tell her his news first.

John told Lucy that his mother was against their dating, and she had asked John to stop dating Lucy and date someone else. Lucy was shocked, and asked John for the reason. John was very frank and told her his mother did not want him to date Puerto Rican girls.

John continued to tell Lucy that his mother did not like Puerto Ricans. She thought they were a lower class people, and the Puerto Rican girls were tramps who were in this country looking to marry nice American men.

Lucy was devastated, and asked John what his plans were. John told her that he loved his mother and did not want to hurt her.

Lucy ran out of the restaurant crying. She was devastated, her dreams, her hopes, her love, all of her plans had just fallen in on her. What was she to do? This was the worst day of her life, now what would she say to her mother, how could she live like this, how could she face life?

The next morning at the breakfast table Lucy did not show. Mom checked her bedroom, and there was no Lucy. She asked Manny and I if we had seen her, Manny and I responded we had not.

I left the table and called John's house, and John told me the last time he had seen Lucy was at The Tree Tavern last evening.

I returned to the table and told the family I had just called John's house, and relayed what John had told me. It was unlike Lucy to go somewhere without telling at least one family member where she was going.

Finally, we all agreed that Lucy probably spent the evening at one of her girlfriend's house. Mom told us she would call Lucy's employer after eight o'clock. Lucy had not missed a day of work for the past year.

Everyone in the family had a bad feeling that something was wrong. That day Mom and Manny both called in sick. They wanted to find Lucy so they could be at peace. I had no choice; I had to go to school, after all it was my senior year and I had to do well.

Mom called Lucy's employer after eight, and was told Lucy was not in. An hour later Mom again called, and the same response was given. Mom called every hour for the next three hours, with the same response.

Calls were placed to most of Lucy's friends at their homes or at their places of employment - no one had seen Lucy.

Mother finally called the Paterson Police Department, and was told that if Lucy did not show up by the next morning, to come to the station and fill out a missing person's report. She was also instructed to bring in a recent photograph of Lucy, all possible information of her girlfriends, boyfriend, employers, and their telephone numbers and addresses.

That evening Manny and I provided Mom with names, addresses and telephone numbers of Lucy's friends, locations Lucy would frequent, and any information we thought might be useful to the police.

Manny had to take a short run for his company in the morning, but would be back early in the afternoon to help.

The next day Lucy had not shown up, so early in the morning Mom went to the Paterson Police Department. She met with Detective Rogers, who would be the detective assigned to work with her. She provided him with all the information he had requested.

He took her telephone number and told her he would be in touch with her on a regular basis, and that if she could think of anything else that could help him with the investigation not to hesitate to call him.

Four days had passed since Lucy's disappearance, and nothing new was learned. Stephanie and I would take long rides searching for Lucy. We drove all through Paterson, West Paterson, Totowa, and other nearby towns. We visited Lucy's friends, neighbors, and anyone we thought may have any information regarding her whereabouts.

Detective Rogers was doing an excellent investigation. He interviewed all of Lucy's friends, her co-workers, our family's friends and neighbors. He especially interviewed John two times, only because John was the last person to see her.

Mom also placed a missing person's ad in the newspapers; she even called her family in Puerto Rico.

I spoke to John. John and I had a good relationship, and we respected each other. He told me about the conversation he had with Lucy the night she disappeared. John held nothing back.

I asked John if he had given this information to Detective Rogers, and John replied, "I did." I asked John if Lucy had told him anything. John said, "I think Lucy did have something to tell me that evening, but after I told her how my mother felt about Puerto Rican girls, and how I didn't want to hurt my mother, Lucy ran out of the restaurant crying."

Even though I was several years younger than John, I gave John some advice. I had heard from others who knew John personally, that he was a "Mama's Boy." I realized this more so after he told me he carried out his mother's wishes regarding Lucy. So, I quoted one of my grandfather's sayings, along with some of my personal thoughts.

"There comes a time when a person has to start to make his own decisions. Mothers are wonderful and look after us. They mean well and are always looking after our welfare. Unfortunately, mothers may not be around forever to guide us. Therefore, future decision making becomes one's responsibility. The decisions you make may differ from your mother's. You will not be hurting her with the decisions you make, you are going one step further. In that step you may be securing your future, and the *best decisions come from the heart."*

At this point, I knew that Lucy did not get a chance to tell John she was pregnant with his child. I did not want to tell him because I knew Lucy wanted to personally tell him. I also believed she should be the one to tell him.

I then put a hypothetical question to John and asked him, "What if Lucy were pregnant, would you marry her?" John quickly responded that he loved Lucy very much and would marry her. I felt very sorry for John.

One week after Lucy's disappearance, Detective Rogers paid our family a visit and told us that they had found Lucy's body. They found it at Garret Mountain, hanging from a tree.

Mom immediately began to cry. We all had a gut feeling that something terrible had happened to her, but now we knew. Manny and I both grabbed Mom and sat her down. Manny and I also had tears in our eyes and great pain in our hearts.

It took a while for us to regain our composure. Detective Rogers was very helpful and extended his condolences to us.

When he thought we were listening, he explained to us that a hunter was exercising his hunting dog and found the body. At this point they were not sure if it was a suicide or a homicide, and that an autopsy would have to be performed this evening to determine what happened to her.

Detective Rogers told us that after the autopsy was completed, the body would be released to the family. If everything went according to schedule, perhaps Lucy's body could be released to the family sometime the following morning.

Lucy's body was released to us early the next morning, and several days later we had her funeral. She was buried next to our grandfather at Calvary Cemetery. Stephanie and her parents attended, as well as many friends and relatives. The repast took place at the Bonfire, a restaurant located on Market Street near the cemetery. At the funeral I thought to myself, "Sometimes life is not fair."

I loved my sister, and for the short years we were together we became very close. All of us had become a close family. I again thought to myself, "Lord, I have lost the two heroes of my life, my grandfather and my father, and now I have lost my sister; what is going to happen next?"

I took Stephanie home, and during the ride I told her that Lucy was pregnant with John's baby. I also told her that as far as I know I am the only one who knows, and asked her not to tell anyone. Stephanie mentioned she would not tell a soul.

Manny felt sure that John had killed our sister, and wanted to beat the truth out of him. I talked to Manny and told him I had spoken to John, and I believed that John would not hurt Lucy because he loved her very much.

I also told Manny that at this point we do not know what happened to Lucy, and we won't know until the results of the autopsy were completed by the Coroner's Office. I also reminded him that Detective Rogers stated the results should be made available to us in a few days.

The next day Detective Rogers met with us and told us that the Coroner's Office had released their autopsy report regarding Lucy's death. They ruled her death a suicide. He also told us that Lucy was pregnant.

Detective Rogers conducted a very thorough investigation. He found the wrappings of the clothes line used. He traced the wrapping to a bodega on Park Avenue. The bodega was very close to the Tree Tavern Restaurant. The bodega's owner identified Lucy's photograph as being the person who had purchased a similar rope on the evening of her disappearance.

Detective Rogers' conclusion was that Lucy doubled the clothes line so it would hold her weight. She securely tied the rope around a large tree. She rolled a large log under the hanging rope to stand on. She tied the rope tightly around her neck, and then pushed the log away with her feet.

The rope did stretch a little with Lucy's weight, but not enough for her to touch the ground. Detective Rogers found two sets of footprints in the area, one set was Lucy's and the other was the hunter's.

After Detective Rogers left, Mom talked to Manny and I. She stated, "I believe that Lucy must have been very depressed, she probably felt rejected, all alone with nobody or no one to turn to, perhaps she had lost all hope, even felt sorry for herself, no matter how bad she felt or what predicament she may have been in, taking her own life was not the answer. What Lucy did was wrong. Her choice to take her own life was a bad choice. She gave up on life. She could have had so much. I want the both of you to know that *no matter how bad things get, there is always a light at the end of the tunnel, there is new life waiting for you. You have to have hope in life and keep a positive attitude and things will turn around for you.* Lucy just gave up. She didn't think of her loved ones, the ones she left behind. Her early departure has left us devastated. It has left us with great grief. We are the ones who have to go on living without her. We are the ones who will keep asking ourselves what could we have done to help her, where did we fail her? Most importantly, taking her life interfered with God's plan, a plan he had worked out for her and each one of us. All we can do now is pray for Lucy, and pray that this never happens again in our family."

The local newspaper printed an article of Lucy's death, but because of Detective Rogers' kindness, the manner of death or Lucy's pregnancy was not mentioned.

At the dinner table that evening, Manny mentioned he still felt that John was responsible for Lucy's death. His conclusion was that he found out she was pregnant, and refused to marry her. As a result she committed suicide.

I told Mom and Manny that I had spoken to John, and John had told me he loved Lucy. I also told them that John was not and is not aware that Lucy was pregnant. If he had known she was, he would have married her.

Moments later John visited us, and spoke with us for some time. John had many tears in his eyes and could not apologize enough. He held himself responsible for her death. He mentioned how much he loved her several times.

John could not attend the funeral, because he had been admitted into St. Joseph's Hospital with a nervous breakdown. John was not aware of Lucy's pregnancy and was never told.

After John left, Manny told Mom and I, "If Tony had not told me that John was unaware of Lucy's pregnancy, I would have beaten him up." I told Manny that hurting John would not bring Lucy back. It would only cause more pain.

I mentioned one of our grandfather's quotes, *"The past is over and we have to recover from the hurts we have experienced. We have to live this new day, have new dreams and make new plans for the future. We have to keep our mistakes in our mind, learn from them and move on."*

Mother kept those words on her mind, but had a difficult time recovering from the hurt she had just gone through. She thought to herself, "Lucy was too young to die; she really didn't get a chance to experience life. Children are supposed to bury their parents, not parents bury their children."

Manny, in his own way still had an attitude towards John. I told Manny, *"Forgiveness is a very powerful tool, and we must learn to forgive.*

Un-forgiveness is a burden upon our shoulders, and will remain there until we forgive." I also told Manny, "John feels responsible for Lucy's death, and John will carry that guilt upon his shoulders until he forgives himself."

I would see John and talk to him on many occasions, and I could see on John's face the guilt he was carrying. Guilt he would carry with him for a long time.

Stephanie and I would visit my grandfather's and Lucy's graves. Stephanie would put fresh flowers on the graves. She always placed three red roses on them in the same format.

I asked Stephanie why she would put three roses on the grave in that particular manner. Stephanie told me the two roses in the V shape represent victory over death, and the center rose represents Jesus. It means victory over death through Jesus.

Stephanie also mentioned that she had learned this format from her Aunt Clara, her mother's sister, who is a Catholic nun, belonging to the order of the Sisters of Atonement, from a place called Graymoor, located in Garrison, New York.

Stephanie told me she doesn't get to see her Aunt Clara often, but they talk on the telephone frequently. Stephanie also told me her Aunt Clara is well informed of our relationship and of the passing of my grandfather and Lucy. Stephanie even mentioned that her Aunt Clara stated she would put fresh roses on their graves when she would visit her relatives who have also been buried there.

That evening Stephanie had been invited by Mom to dine with us, and after dinner I drove her home. In route to her house, Stephanie noticed the rosary beads my mom had given to me on my confirmation day, hanging on my rear view mirror. I had found them in my dresser drawer and hung them up that same day. She took them down, looked at them closely, and told me how beautiful they were.

I told her my mom had given them to me when I made my confirmation. I told her if she wanted them I would give them to her. She said, "No, they are a special gift for you from your mom. I can't take them."

I told Stephanie I would give them to her when we got married, then we can both use them. Her response was, "That's a lovely idea." The next day I took the rosary beads to the jewelers and had them engraved. The name Stephanie Mullen was etched on them. Afterwards I placed them back on my mirror.

One evening I was invited to dine at the Mullens' house. At the dinner table Mr. Mullen asked me where I would be attending college and what was to be my field of study. I told him I wanted to attend Rutgers University, and study electrical engineering. Mr. Mullen responded that electrical engineering was an excellent choice. He suggested I should try to minor in business, just in case I ever wanted to start my own business.

Mr. Mullen told me that he had an electrical engineering degree with a minor in business, and was using both of those disciplines in his new company. He mentioned he would be leaving the newspaper business in a few weeks, and would be working full-time at his new company.

Mr. Mullen continued by saying that electrical engineering is the future of the country, and the country would need engineers to provide the government with technology to support their space program.

The minor in business helped him in starting up his new business. A business that would provide the required equipment, the parts, and other miscellaneous items needed to make our space program a reality.

Mr. Mullen then made me a job offer; he said, "After you graduate from school, come and see me. I can use good men in my company."

After dinner Stephanie and I sat at the front porch. Stephanie told me her father's business was very successful, that he had received several government contracts, and would be purchasing a bigger building to house more employees. She also told me that her parents would be purchasing a larger home somewhere outside the city of Paterson. I told Stephanie that my mother had found two houses she was interested in purchasing. One was located in the Lakeview section of Paterson, and the other in Totowa, N.J.

My next question was, "What does your father think about me?" Stephanie replied, "I think he likes you, he took you sailing and let you sail his prize sailboat. He invited you over for our family picnics. It was his idea to have you over for dinner, and even offered you a job. You are the son he never had."

While we were on the subject of sons, I asked Stephanie why her parents never had other children. She said that her mom had many complications during childbirth, and resulted in her not being able to have any more children.

I then asked her, "Does your father like children?" Her reply was he loves them and told me he wants at least three grandchildren.

I told Stephanie, "I also like your father." Stephanie further mentioned that in a few weeks her father was going to have someone take the sailboat to Martha's Vineyard to have the woodwork inside the boat refurbished.

Her father was going to ask his cousin Michael to take the boat for the repairs, and he wants someone to sail with Michael. "He was thinking of asking you, he believes you are very careful with your personal property, reliable and a pretty good sailor."

Stephanie graduated St. Joseph's High School, and for her graduation present her parents brought her a new 1956 Chevrolet, Chinese red top and white bottom, two door hardtop convertible.

Stephanie was accepted into Mount St. Mary College in Bethesda, Maryland. Her major would be in English, and her goal was to one day teach English at an elementary school.

I graduated Eastside several days after Stephanie graduated St. Joseph's. I did have to change my plans. I would no longer be attending Rutgers University because I was given a partial scholarship to Massachusetts Institute of Technology. I would, as planned, be majoring in electrical engineering, with a minor in business.

Stephanie had requested that the first page of my yearbook be reserved for her. The first chance she got she wrote in it. "Tony, our love was a flame meant to be before we were born. We both lit that flame when we first met. Let's keep it burning for all eternity." It was signed Forever yours, Stephanie.

Stephanie and I were invited to my classmate Jay's graduation party. Jay and I remained the best of friends throughout our school years. During his senior year, Jay's parents, who were financially well off, bought Jay a 1956 fire engine red Pontiac Bonneville.

Jay would drive his new car to school, because his parents had moved from Paterson, N.J. to a very wealthy community in North Caldwell, N.J. Jay's father owned a financial institution called The Pearlman Group, an investment company located on Wall Street, in New York City. Jay would be attending New York University and would be majoring in business administration; after graduation Jay would be co-owner of his father's company.

Jay's graduation party was the best party we attended. It was held at Jay's house, which had a grand ball room. In this room there were ten tables that each sat eight people. The food was catered by a very fine restaurant, and the music was provided by a live band. The company was also nice, and we all had a wonderful time. Stephanie and I enjoyed ourselves. We laughed and danced all night.

Jay was still dating Ann, and they had made plans to marry after they graduated from college. Ann would be attending Sherwood Business School, and had plans on becoming a secretary.

Stephanie started school two weeks before me, so I was able to drive her there in her new car. She did not want her car at school for the first semester. After the trip I would return her car to her parent's house. The trip took five hours, and we had plenty of time to talk about our past and our future.

I asked Stephanie what she thought of me when she first met me. She replied, "I thought you were cute, and a little shy, especially the way you disappeared when I told you I knew your name from being in my Ancient History class, and the way you disappeared the second time we spoke, when you blurted out I was beautiful."

I told her the reason I darted out the nearest door was because I was embarrassed. "I really wanted to get to know you, and walk you home." We both laughed.

I told her, "I was devastated when you did not show up for school. I was unaware of your transfer to St. Joseph's." Stephanie said, "I was also upset because I wanted to tell you I was going to transfer to another school, and give you my telephone number, but on that day you were absent from class."

I asked her why she had transferred from Eastside to St. Joseph's. She replied that Eastside was a large school and she wanted to attend a smaller school; she also wanted a Catholic education.

I asked her if the transfer was her parent's idea. She said, "No, it was my idea. I applied, and when I was accepted I told my parents I wanted to attend."

We talked about how our lives would be changing, our parents buying new homes, we would both be attending new schools, new friends, but most importantly we would be apart from each other. We were accustomed to seeing each other just about every day. We would miss doing things together and just being in each other's company.

We were not afraid of these new changes, because we knew that the love we had for each other was real and strong. We also made tentative arrangements to marry after we both graduated from college.

Stephanie told me, "Tony you are the only one in my life, if anything should happen to you or to our relationship I would never marry." She believed she could never have the same relationship or feel this way towards anyone else. I responded, "I feel the same way you do, but regardless of what happens the most important thing is that you are happy. That is what I mostly want for you, and I believe we will both be very happy together."

We arrived at her school and I helped her get settled. I met her roommate, and jotted down Stephanie's new telephone number; which was a public telephone in the hallway. She instructed me, "When you call, give the person who answers my name and room number, and please wait, it might take some time."

Before I left, Stephanie asked me, "When you drop off the car, could you please pick up your graduation ring? I took it off to shower and left it on top of my dresser. Then could you mail it to me, I have already begun to miss it." Stephanie always wore my ring around her neck on a gold chain I gave her for her birthday. She jotted down her school address for me on a piece of paper where I could mail it to her.

I kissed her goodbye, hugged her, and squeezed her hand. We would deeply miss each other. We would not meet again until the Christmas vacation.

With much sadness I departed for my long journey home. I thought how much I would miss her, this would be the first time we would not see each other for many weeks. I did have her graduation photo in my wallet, which would become for me my new companion.

On my journey I thought of the wonderful times we had together. I had become part of her family and she had become part of mine. I could not wait to see her again.

I dropped off Stephanie's car at her parents' house. It was very late when I arrived, and I did not want to awaken her parents. I thought I would get the ring on my next visit to the Mullen's house.

I left Stephanie's car in their driveway. I parked it in her parking spot, locked the car and took the keys with me. The keys were my personal set given to me by Stephanie. I was aware that her parents had their own set. Afterwards, I departed for home in my old but trusty jalopy, which I had parked on the street prior to our departure.

I received my first card from Stephanie several days later. It was a greeting card with a picture of a young man and young woman walking in a garden and holding hands. On the top was written, "Miss you." Inside the card she wrote. "Tony, I began to miss you the moment you left. I can't wait until we graduate so we can be together forever. It was signed Forever yours, Stephanie." Her card was short and sweet and I shall treasure it for the rest of my life.

Chapter Five

"No, Not Again"

I had two weeks at home before I would depart to my new school. One evening Mr. Mullen called me and asked me if I could have dinner with him and his wife. I indicated I could.

After dinner, Mr. Mullen asked me if I was available to take his sailboat to Martha's Vineyard, to have the inside refurbished. He told me his cousin Michael was sailing the boat there, but needed someone to accompany him.

It would take about one week to sail there, have the work completed, and return. He would pay me $300 for the trip, and he assured me that Michael was an excellent sailor.

I asked him if it would be okay for me to get back to him with an answer. I was available, and I could use the money. However, I just wanted to notify my mother and brother in case they had something planned.

I checked with my family and they had no plans, so I called Mr. Mullen and told him I was available. He thanked me and told me that Michael and I would be leaving this coming Sunday.

Saturday evening just after dinner, I called Stephanie at school. As Stephanie had mentioned, it took several minutes before she was able to respond to my call. I told Stephanie I had dinner with her parents, and her father had asked me to sail "Stephanie" to Martha's Vineyard with Michael. We would be leaving early tomorrow morning.

I apologized to her for forgetting to get her ring from her dresser and mailing it to her. I told her upon my return from our trip to her school, I arrived late at her house and I did not want to awaken her parents. After dinner tonight, I just forgot. I assured her that upon my return form Martha's Vineyard I shall pick up the ring and mail it to her.

On Sunday, at 4:00 in the morning, I was picked up at my house by Mr. Mullen. We drove to the marina where we met Michael. Michael was several years younger than Mr. Mullen. He was a very likeable and dependable person.

Michael and I got along very well; he was an excellent sailor, had a very good sense of humor and very witty. The trip would be fun. We had plenty of food and drinks for the journey.

Mr. Mullen gave Michael the necessary papers, maps, keys, money for the trip, and last minute instructions. Afterwards Michael and I departed on our journey.

We arrived at Martha's Vineyard late Monday evening. Early the next day we met with the people who would be doing the repairs. They started working on the boat immediately.

The boat would be our home for the next week. We would eat and sleep on it. However, Stephanie's father, who was well organized, made prior arrangements, in case it was necessary for us to stay at a nearby motel. This meant if we could not stand the smell of the newly applied paint, or if our presence were to interfere with the repairs, we would stay at a motel.

During the repairs we would go swimming, fishing, and eat out at the local restaurants. It was a very enjoyable trip. I mostly enjoyed watching the tuna boats docking with their freshly caught fish. They would pull their fishing boats to shore, where there would be lines of either refrigerated trucks or trucks filled with ice. The trucks were from restaurants or fish markets, and the drivers were waiting to purchase the yellow fin tuna. The fish was inspected, hung on a large scale, and the buyer would pay hundreds of dollars in cash for the tuna. The fish weighed several hundred pounds.

The work on "Stephanie" was completed on time and we made our journey back to New Jersey. We arrived back to the marina on Sunday as planned, and I had just three days to pack before I headed to my new school.

At the marina, we secured the boat. Michael gave me the keys and the necessary paper for me to give to Mr. Mullen. Michael had to hurry back home, and asked me to tell Mr. Mullen if he would call him during the evening hours. He was picked up by his wife and children. I greeted his family and thanked Michael for a wonderful time. I waited a short time before Mr. Mullen arrived.

Mr. Mullen arrived and appeared to be very sad. His eyes were droopy and puffy, and had dark colored rings around them. He greeted me, put his arm around my shoulders, and asked me to walk with him.

I could sense that something was wrong. He then proceeded to tell me he had bad news for me. He told me the news, and when I heard it I could not believe it, I asked him to repeat it again.

I wasn't sure if I didn't hear it right, or if I just didn't want to hear it. He told me the news again and it sunk in, I had heard it correctly just as he said it the first time. My eyes filled with tears, I got a lump in my throat, a knot in my stomach, and my knees became weak. My knees finally gave out and I fell to my knees, and said to myself "No, not again."

He told me that Stephanie had been hit and killed by a car while she was walking on campus. She had been killed the day after Michael and I departed for our trip. He tried to notify us, but the person working on the boat was not at his shop, because he was working on the boat. He tried to get numbers of other nearby marinas and vendors, but was unsuccessful.

Stephanie had been buried on Thursday at Holy Sepulcher Cemetery in Totowa, N.J. The saddest day of my life was here. My whole life was now changed, nothing else mattered. How could I go on living without her?

Mr. Mullen told me, "Stephanie always talked about you, she would tell me what a wonderful person you are, and how well you both got along. She loved you very much. She told me one of the best things about you was that you made her very happy."

He also told me, "I can imagine how you feel. I felt the same way when I received the news. If there is something I can do for you, please let me know, you have my telephone number and you are always welcome at our house."

On the way home I asked Mr. Mullen if he would take me to visit her gravesite. On the way, I asked him to stop at a florist so I could pick up some flowers for Stephanie's grave. We stopped at a florist, where I picked up three red roses. When we arrived, I placed the flowers on her gravesite in the same format she used to put flowers on Lucy's and my grandfather's graves.

Mr. Mullen drove me home, and on the way I asked him how his wife was doing, and he told me she was very upset. She had visited the doctor and he had prescribed some medication to help her relax. I asked him to give her my condolences.

Mr. Mullen also gave me my graduation ring. He said, "Stephanie called me the day you departed for Martha's Vineyard, and asked me to give to you this ring. I believed she wanted you to mail it to her." He also stated, "I think Stephanie would want you to have it as a reminder of her, and the relationship you two had." I thanked him and told him it meant a lot to me.

I arrived at home and told Mother and Manny the news. I knew they had not heard, because Mr. Mullen told me he tried to contact them, but was unable. Mom and Manny had tears in their eyes. Their tears were for me because they knew how much Stephanie meant to me.

Mom told me one of Grandfather's quotes, a quote he had mailed to me in one of his letters. She said, *"We have to accept life as it is; sometimes it is good, sometime it is hurtful, painful and full of sorrow, try to do the best with what you have left."*

I asked Mom. "What do I have left?" She replied, "You have your family who loves you very much, you have your education, you have your faith, and you have a life to live ahead of you." Mom also stated, *"Tony, you have to look to the future, because that is where you will be spending the rest of your life, and your future starts now. Your future will be what you make it."*

Manny told me, "It's going to be hard, but I have faith in you. I know in time you will bounce back. Mom and I will be here for you." I hugged them both and we cried together.

I was sad, tired, weak and hungry. I could not eat because my stomach was upset. The only thing for me to do was to rest. As I lay in bed the only thing I could think of was Stephanie.

The next day nothing had changed; I still had that ache in my stomach and the knot in my throat. I had brown circles under my eyes, and my eyes themselves were red from the many tears I shed during that evening.

During our early breakfast, Mom and Manny took me outside and gave me a graduation present. They had bought me a 1954 Chevrolet, two tone green. I was very thankful. I would have been elated with their present if it were not for the ache I had in my heart.

I deeply thanked them and gave them each a big hug. The car was beautiful. If I were to pick my own car out, it would have been the one they gave me. Mom told me, "You are going to a very good school, Manny and I think you should have a very good start, and this car is a part of that good start; besides you need a little cheering up."

Later that morning I checked our mail box, which was located on our front porch. In the box I received an envelope from Mr. Mullen. He must have delivered it personally because it did not contain a postage stamp.

Inside the envelope there was three hundred dollars. The envelope also contained a note from Mr. Mullen. The note read. "Tony, with all the sad feelings we both experienced yesterday, I forgot to pay you for taking my boat to Martha's Vineyard. I not only want to thank you for the boat, but most importantly I want to thank you for taking care of Stephanie, and making her so happy for the past four years". It was signed - Dad Mullen.

I again developed tears in my eyes. I went upstairs and shared the note with Mom. Mom had taken off from work to be with me during my crisis. She was very thoughtful and was there for me. She told me, *"Tony your mind is a very powerful tool. Whatever you think and you believe, you will become. Your mind also holds emotions. If emotions are not used properly, they can hinder your true self."*

I asked her, "Mom, how can I ever forget Stephanie?" Mom said, "I am not asking you to forget Stephanie. Stephanie will always be with you in your memory, as a living truth which just passed. I am asking you to count the feeling you had for each other as good memories."

I spent much of that day at the Motor Vehicle Department located on Market Street, near Public School Number 24. Afterwards, I took the car to get inspected. I washed it and made sure it was mechanically sound. Even though I was busy, I still had Stephanie on my mind.

I telephoned Jay and asked him if he wanted to meet me. He replied, "My house or yours?" I told him I wanted to take a ride, so I suggested we meet at his house. We met and I asked him if he had heard the news about Stephanie, and he responded he did not. I told him what had happened to her.

Jay was saddened and immediately called his girlfriend Ann. When Ann heard the news she was surprised and began to cry. Jay asked why he and Ann were not contacted, and I told them because I had been away. I also told him it happened suddenly and her parents wished not to publicize it.

I showed Jay my new car and we drove to Bon's Ice Cream Parlor in Montclair, N.J. to get an Awful – Awful (large ice cream shakes.) If you can drink two, you get the third one for free.

Jay and I talked, and he told me he would be starting school the coming week. I drove Jay home, and before we departed he told me if I needed anything while I was at school to call him. He further stated he would be coming home on weekends from school, and to contact him at his parent's home in about two weeks. He also stated he would be living off-campus and would have a telephone at his off-campus residence. He currently did not have the number but would provide it to me when I called.

The next day I had to pack for school, and made sure I had my school packet handy. I placed the packet in my glove compartment to have it readily available. I had obtained it when I attended orientation day. The packet contained my school schedule, school maps, classroom locations, the name of my dorm and dorm room number, and temporary identification to get onto school grounds.

I would be departing the next day and needed to arrive before four o'clock, so I could pick up the necessary keys, my school photo identification and a parking permit. I went to bed early that evening so I could have an early start in the morning.

That evening I had a lot on my mind; I thought about the new school I would be attending, new classmates, my new roommate. I knew his name was Raymond Rooney, who was also majoring in engineering, but I had not met him. However, in the center of my thoughts was Stephanie.

I thought of how wonderful our lives would have been. I could never meet someone like her, or have the relationship we had. The only saving grace I now have is what Mom had told me.

Mom told me to enjoy the wonderful memories we had together. That is just what I am going to do. When I think of her and feel sad, I will think of a cherished moment we once had and treasure that moment.

Very early the next morning Mom, Manny and I got up early and had breakfast together. Before I departed, Mom said, "Tony this is a great opportunity for you. We are very proud of you and what you have accomplished, and we know that you will continue to make us proud."

Manny said, "Little brother, I know what you are capable of. I know that *if you set your mind to it, you can do anything you want to*. Do it for us, for Mom, for me, for Lucy, and for Stephanie." I kissed and hugged them and left.

I finally departed for school, and during my long drive I had plenty of time to think. The first thought that came into my mind was one of my grandfather's quotes. He had told me, *"When you are alone and have time to spare, don't waste it. Time is very valuable. Use the time to make plans and evaluate your life."*

I started to think about my life. Grandfather had given me clues on how to begin. He said, *"Think about where you have been. What you have done or failed to do. Ask yourself where could I have done better? Is there anything that needs to be changed? Did I hurt anyone; if so, is forgiveness needed?"*

In my evaluation I thought about the past. As far as I can recall, everything seemed to be in order. I hadn't hurt anyone, and I didn't make any major mistakes. I did forget to visit Mrs. Mullen to give her my condolences, and asked her how she was feeling. However, I will visit her on my return home during my first school break.

The next part of Grandfather's quote was, *"Think of the future, ask yourself what are my goals in life and what do I need to do to get there?"* For my future, I want to finish school and I want to give it an all-out effort to do my best. After all, my grandfather always stressed how important an education is. Besides, I want to do it for myself, for Mom and Manny. They have always been there for me and continue to encourage me.

After graduation I would look for employment within my field, perhaps I might take up Mr. Mullen's job offer. When the name Mullen came to mind I thought of Stephanie.

Stephanie and I had planned to marry. My next question was what would now be my plan, as far as matrimony is concerned?

I remembered Stephanie's vow, that if something should happen to me she would never marry. I then made up my mind, so it will be for me. There could never be another Stephanie, so there would never be another woman in my life. I will honor what Stephanie vowed to do.

The last part of my grandfather's quote was, *"Most important in your life should be your faith. Try to keep it alive, and constantly evaluate it to make sure it continues to grow."*

The last part of Grandfather's quote was the hardest for me, only because I had been questioning God regarding all of the things which have happened in my life. As a young boy I buried my father, but during the past year I have buried my grandfather, my sister, and Stephanie.

As I talked to God I told him, "I don't blame You for what has happened." I said this because my grandfather had once told me, *"Don't blame God for whatever happens in your life. Blame yourself and others, because God has given us a great gift, a gift of freewill. There will come times when we and others make bad decisions in our lives. When we do, it may affect us and others negatively. However, it is then that God will bring good out of the bad choices we have made."* My question to God is what good has come out of all of the mishaps in my life?

I thought of possible answers. As far as my father's death was concerned, it was his choice to join the military, a choice which prematurely took his life. Where has God brought good out of his bad choice? Perhaps it was a factor which caused us to move to America, where we could have a better life. Also, it gave me the opportunity to be raised by my grandfather, who has given me a preparation into what a good life should be.

What good has God brought out of my grandfather's death? My evaluation of his death is that my grandfather had lived a good life, and had been a good example to everyone he had touched.

I am not sure, but perhaps Lucy's death may have helped other young girls her age, maybe one of her girlfriends, or maybe John. The struggle

I am having is Stephanie. I cannot think of any good that has come out of her death. Maybe the future may have an answer for me, but for now I am perplexed.

I arrived at school in time to grab a late lunch at the cafeteria. I took an empty seat next to a young man I thought might be a freshman. I was right, he was a freshman. He was also Ray Rooney, my roommate, what a coincidence.

Ray was average height, with light brown hair, light brown eyes, medium complexion and medium build. He was very pleasant and a happy individual. We ate, talked, and got acquainted with each other. We shared common interests, such as our educational goals. We both had received good grades in high school, partial scholarships, and both of us were majoring in engineering. I was very pleased to have Ray as a roommate.

After lunch we registered and received our school identification, parking permits, and room keys. Afterwards, we proceeded to our dorm. Our room was located on the second floor, and was one of the larger rooms. It had two single beds, two large dressers, two desks, and a window facing out towards the front of the building. Ray and I were pleased with our room because it was located at the end of the hallway, which was away from the stairs, and would give us some peace and quiet from scrambling students.

We unpacked our suitcases and got settled. The first thing I placed on the top of my dresser was Stephanie's picture. Ray asked, "Who's the pretty young woman?" I told him the story of Stephanie and me, and what had happened to her.

Ray was sympathetic and understanding. Ray's first item to be placed on the top of his dresser was a photo of his girlfriend. Her name was Donna and she had been in Ray's graduating class. They were both from a small town called Cuba, New York. They had been dating for two years and they planned to marry after Ray's graduation. Donna was recently employed as a secretary with the Palace Hotel in Olean, New York, a town several miles from Cuba, N.Y.

Ray and I reviewed our class schedules, and we were in three of the same classes: mathematics, physics, and English. We toured the school grounds in an attempt to get acquainted with the layout. We also located the buildings where our classes would be held.

Chapter Six

"Reconstruction Days"

The freshman class was told that about a minimum of fifteen percent of the class would drop out, transfer, or fail. The school administrators told us that their curriculum would be at a rapid pace, and recommended that study groups would be a great asset to us.

Ray and I decided that the fewer study groups we were in, the better it would be for us. Being in many study groups may interfere with each other, and would require more of our time. So we devised a plan to select the most difficult subjects we thought may require a study group. We came up with math and physics.

Our last class was physics, and after our classes Ray and I asked some of the students who were in our math and physic classes to form a study group. The group consisted of Joseph Palumbo, a young man from Central High School in Paterson, New Jersey. I had seen Joe play at many basketball games when Eastside played against Central, but I was never formally introduced to him. From my recollection, Joe was an excellent basketball player.

In conversing with Joe, I learned he had aspirations of playing basketball for MIT. Joe was a mechanical engineering major, and had received above average grades in high school, but did extremely well in his SAT Scores. He was tall, had a slender build, black hair and brown eyes.

The second member of our study group was Mary Bentley. She was a very beautiful young woman from Roxbury, Connecticut. Mary had long light brown hair, hazel/green eyes, and fair complexion with a thin build. Mary was from a wealthy family in Connecticut. Their wealth came from the retailing business. Mary was a chemistry major, and was awarded a full academic scholarship. Mary was also in our math, physics, and English classes.

Our third study group member was James McCoy. Jim was from Brooklyn, New York. Jim was average height, had brown hair, blue eyes, and a medium build. Jim was majoring in mechanical engineering and was an excellent high school student.

Ray was the fourth study group member and I the fifth. After introductions, we shared our room numbers and proceeded to the cafeteria to dine and get better acquainted.

Our classes were, as we were told at our orientation, at a very rapid pace, and the study groups were very beneficial to all. Our study group was well attended and orderly. It seemed that all participants had the same goal – good grades. Mary and I controlled the group. I believe it was because she and I put extra effort into our studies, and when asked questions, we usually came up with the right answers.

Our study group meetings were held in available classrooms, study halls, the cafeteria, and if none of these were available we would have them in our dorm room. Ray and I volunteered our dorm room because it was the quietest, and largest dorm.

Mary tried to sit next to me, I believed because most of the questions were usually directed at us. Thanksgiving break came by quickly. It was a four-day break, including the weekend, and many students who lived within driving distance went home for the holiday. Everyone in our study group was going home except for Mary.

After one of our classes, I asked Mary why she wasn't going home for the Thanksgiving break. She responded she wanted to go home but she had brought her car to be serviced, and due to a heavy volume of repairs, her vehicle would not be ready in time.

I asked her if I could drive her home. She indicated she did not want to inconvenience me. I insisted and we plotted out a route. It would only take me just a little over one hour extra to drive her home.

We made arrangements to leave early in the morning. The trip was pleasurable and we arrived at her very large and beautiful home. Her home had six bedrooms, of which four were guest rooms, five full-sized bathrooms, a main kitchen, and a larger kitchen near the great room. The great room was used as a ballroom. The house had a library, a game room, and plenty of storage space. It was set on twenty acres, of which ten was taken up by a fishing pond. They also had an Olympic-sized swimming pool, and a smaller home which was the living quarters of a married couple who were their house maid and groundskeeper.

Her parents greeted us and invited me to lunch with them. They were very nice, pleasant and welcoming. After lunch, her mom forced me to take a soft drink and fruit for the rest of my journey. I departed and was eager to get to my new residence.

After I left, Mary's mom asked Mary, "He seems like a very nice young man, are you two dating"? Mary responded, "Not yet."

My home was now in Totowa, New Jersey. Mom had purchased that one family house she dreamed about. She had written to me and told me all about the house. Mom and Manny had tried to arrange everything in my room as it was in our old house.

The house was located on Crescent Court, a few blocks from Union Boulevard. The house had a full basement with a recreational room and a bathroom, a master bedroom, a living room, kitchen, and dining room on the first floor, two bedrooms, a study and a bathroom on the second floor. It had a one car attached garage and a nice big yard.

Mom was very proud of her house and had it nicely decorated. Mom took the first floor bedroom, and Manny and I had the two second floor bedrooms. Manny gave me the largest bedroom, because he had plans of marrying soon.

Mom and Manny had done a marvelous job arranging my room. It was exactly as it was in the old house. After I was able to get settled, I picked up the telephone and called the Mullens. I called to see if they were going to be at home. I wanted to visit them to find out how Mrs. Mullen was doing. I also wanted to give her my condolences.

A strange woman picked up the telephone, and told me the Mullens had moved. I had forgotten that Stephanie told me her parents were buying a larger house outside the City of Paterson.

I asked the woman if the Mullens had left a forwarding address or telephone number. The woman responded she had dealt with a realty company, and had only seen the Mullens the day she bought the house.

The woman kindly provided me with the name of the realty company. I called information and obtained the telephone number and called them. A real estate agent answered and after my inquiry, the agent provided me with Mr. Mullen's old telephone number at the newspaper. The agent also told me that this was the only number they had for the Mullens.

Mom invited Gladys and her parents to dine with us. Mom wanted to get better acquainted with the future in-laws. Even though we had a full house, and there was plenty of activity and good food to eat, I felt lonely. It was my first holiday without Stephanie.

I was able to visit Jay. He and I had communicated and made arrangements to meet briefly for an update on our new schools, friends and family. The holidays went by quickly, and back at school, Mary, Ray and I became very good friends. Mary would sit next to us in the cafeteria, at sporting events, and at other social functions.

After a study group session, which was held at our dorm, Mary quietly asked Ray if the pictures on top of our dressers were of our girlfriends. Ray replied, "Yes." From that day on, Mary no longer sat next to us at our study groups, and she wasn't as warm as she had been before.

One day Mary got Ray on the side and asked Ray if he was serious about his girlfriend, and Ray replied that he and his girl had made tentative plans to marry after his graduation. She then asked how about me and my girlfriend? Ray told Mary about Stephanie's death. Mary commented, "Oh, what a shame," but had a slight smile on her face.

From that day on, Mary once again became warm towards us, and would sit next to us during our study group sessions. She never come right out and asked us to go out with her, but she would ask, "Are you guys going to the concert, game, or the play on such a date?" As a result, she, Ray and I ended up sitting next to each other.

Keeping to the vow I made to myself about never marrying, I never led Mary on. I did enjoy her company, and we became very good friends. Ray did tell me about her inquiries regarding Stephanie. Ray believed Mary might be falling in love with me.

One day Mary and I were alone, and I asked her what she thought about me. Her response was, "Why?" I told her that Ray had a feeling that maybe you were falling in love with me. She asked me, "What do you think?" I told her that I never gave it any thought, until Ray mentioned it. I did tell her that I thought she was very beautiful, intelligent, and would make someone very happy. I also told her that under normal conditions, I would be very happy if it were true.

Clever as she was, she asked me, "What do you mean under normal conditions?" I told her about the relationship I had with Stephanie, and how I am not ready to start dating at this time. She was very understanding, but she never answered my question about possibly falling in love with me.

That night I thought to myself, I wasn't very frank with Mary. I should have told her about the vow I made to myself. Was I beginning to have doubts about my vow? Was I beginning to fall in love with Mary, after all she is very pleasant, intelligent, has a good sense of humor and is very beautiful?"

I have learned from my grandfather that *telling the truth is a great quality, and will always work out for the best interest of all.* So, I decided not to lead her on into a one-way love affair. I will speak to her in the morning and tell her about my vow.

The next day I had the opportunity to be alone with Mary. I apologized to her for not being frank with her. She asked me, "Frank about what?" I told her that I after the relationship I had with Stephanie, I made a vow to myself that there would ever be anyone else in my life.

Mary cleverly said, "So, you think I am interested in you?" I responded, "I really don't know. If you are interested, I am flattered. If not, you make it easier for me." She asked me, "How do you feel about me?" I told her, "I think you know the answer to that question. This is why I'm telling you about my vow."

I asked Mary, "Are you falling in love with me?" Her response was, "You know the answer to that question, that's why you told me about your vow." We both skirted the issue about any one of us being in love with the other.

Mary and I continued to be very good friends and continued to go to various places together, but we would not mention love, never embraced or kissed each other, just great friends.

One day Mary spoke to Ray, and had him swear to complete secrecy, after which Ray told her his lips were sealed. Mary proceeded to tell him that she was in love with me, and has loved me ever since the day she had met me.

Mary continued by telling Ray, when she saw Stephanie's picture on top of his dresser she was heartbroken. Then she found out that Stephanie had died in a car accident, and her heart was once again set on fire. Now she found out I had made a vow to not fall in love again. Mary told Ray, "I feel like I'm on a love roller coaster."

Ray told Mary he was aware of my vow, and asked Mary if I had ever told her that I loved her. Mary responded, no, that is why I am here to ask you. Has he ever mentioned anything to you about me?

Ray told Mary that Tony is at times hard to read, but he will look for signs and let her know. Ray also told Mary not to give up. If you love him, and he loves you he may break that vow. Remember Stephanie was his first love, and he may be having difficulties getting over her death. Furthermore, things change, people change, and circumstances change.

Ray was going to tell me about his conversation he had with Mary, but Ray knew me and how I felt about being honest. He remembered me telling him that *a man's word is very valuable.* Therefore, Ray decided not to break his word to Mary.

Ray did ask me what I thought about Mary, I told him that Mary and I are great friends. Ray then asked me if I had not made that vow, would I ever consider dating Mary. I told Ray, "If I had not made my vow, Mary would be an excellent choice. It would be very easy to love her."

Our first year went by quickly, and with the hard work Mary, Ray, and I put into our studies, we were rewarded with all As. Jim received four As and a B in his biology class, and Joe received three Bs and two Cs.

During my summer break I promised myself I would spend my time relaxing, and enjoying myself. Jay, who had received excellent grades from NYU, felt the same way. He and I would go to Fairlawn Bathing Beach Swimming Pool and just relax, enjoy the good weather, and have fun.

One day, while we were enjoying ourselves at the bathing beach, Jay asked me if I was dating anyone. I told him I was not, and I told him about my vow not to marry. I also told him that I was very close to a girl named Mary, but I felt my vow is more important. Jay responded by saying, "That's a crazy idea." He continued to tell me, "I hope someday you will change your mind."

Jay then gave me some of my words of wisdom I had shared with him one of our conversations years ago. He stated, "I just hope by your commitment, you do not pass up a good opportunity. Opportunities may only come up once in our lifetime, don't pass up a good one."

On one of our pool visits, Jay brought Ann. Ann told me Jay had mentioned to her about my vow. Ann said, "Tony, I know you are a person of your word, and once you make a promise you keep it, but the vow you made is a very big commitment and it will definitely affect your life forever." I told her I was well aware of it.

I tried to locate the Mullens, but I had no luck. I went to the newspaper where he once worked. They stated they had no forwarding telephone number or an address for him. I believed they may have the information, but won't give it out. I tried to locate him by inquiring on recent businesses that had been started in the county, but there were many, and I did not know the name of his new company. Jay's father tried to help me locate him by using his business contacts. He even tried the newspaper - to no avail.

I would not give up. I would continue my search. I even visited Stephanie's grave more often, hoping I might see one of the Mullens there. Each visit I would purchase three red roses and place them in the same format used by Stephanie.

Summer ended quickly, and just before I returned to school Mom asked me how I was doing. I answered with a question. I asked her, "In what way?" The reason for my question was because she knew I had received excellent grades in school. She was also aware that Jay and I had an enjoyable summer.

Mom softly replied, "How are you doing socially?" I told her I had made many new friends at school. Mom then came right out and asked me if I was dating anyone. Mom knew the answer to that question, because if I were dating someone, I would have written to her and told her.

I told her I had several female friends, but I am not dating any of them. Mom asked me if I still think about Stephanie, and I told her yes, I think of her often.

Manny, who was in the room, told me, "Under normal circumstances, and as time passes, you will think of her less often. Just try to remember the most treasured memories." Manny continued, "That's what I try to do when I think about Lucy."

I told them about my personal vow. Mom's reply was, "At your age, that is a very hard vow to keep, you probably made it because of the feelings you had for Stephanie. Your feelings may have been right at the time, however, *with age and wisdom, people change and their feelings change.* Therefore, you should keep your options open in that area. If you should change your mind, it will be okay to do so." She continued, "Besides I would like to have many grandchildren."

Manny's response was, "About that vow that you made, I hope you change your mind. When you do, choose another girl wisely, and don't be comparing her to Stephanie."

Everyone in my family, and my friends, were against my vow. They don't know how I felt about Stephanie and the wonderful times and relationship we had.

Mom mentioned she had visited Stephanie's grave, and also tried to call the Mullens to see how they were doing, but the number had been changed. I told Mom that they had moved about the same time we moved, and I was in the process of trying to locate them.

I returned to school and got right back into the study mode. We kept our study group alive, Ray, Mary and I continued going to social events together. Mary and I did not mention love nor tried to keep our relationship above good friends.

Thanksgiving break was a short break, so Ray and I made arrangements to stay on campus and eat at a nearby restaurant. Mary, whose parents were coming to visit the campus, asked me if I wanted to join her and her parents at a nearby restaurant for Thanksgiving dinner. I politely thanked her and told her Ray and I had made prior arrangements.

Christmas season arrived, and most students went home for the holidays. Mary had asked me to stop at her house on my way back to school. I felt bad refusing her invitation, because I had refused to join her and her parent for Thanksgiving dinner. So, I said yes, and that I would call her when I left my parents' home.

At our house Mom and Manny made arrangements for the annual family reunion. All of our family members who resided in New Jersey and New York were invited. Gladys's family was also invited.

We were all in a wonderful Christmas spirit. Dinner was about to begin, and Mom had just finished saying grace, when Manny got on his knees and said to Gladys, "Gladys I love you very much, will you marry me?" Gladys, with tears in her eyes quickly responded, "Yes I will."

Manny had already asked and received permission from Gladys' parents to marry their daughter, and Mom had been previously consulted and had given Manny her blessing. Everyone applauded and was happy to hear the good news.

Manny quickly slipped a beautiful engagement ring on Gladys' finger. More tears came from Gladys's eyes, and more applause was given to them. After dinner we opened Christmas presents and shared old family stories, many which had been shared during previous family gatherings.

Manny got me on the side and asked me to be his best man. I told him it would be an honor. Manny also said, "Tony, I think it would be a great idea if you could bring a date." I knew Manny was trying to help me get Stephanie off my mind. My response to him was, "I'll see what I can do."

Gladys and Manny had set a tentative date of Saturday, June 21, for their wedding. Manny also told me that he was going to invite Jay and Ann. Manny knew them both from their frequent visits to our house, and was also aware of the close friendship Jay and I had. My thought at the time was, perhaps Manny was telling me he was inviting Jay and Ann in an attempt to encourage me to bring a date.

On my way back to school I called Mary and told her I was leaving my house, and gave her an estimation of the time of my arrival. The day before I had purchased a beautiful fruit basket for her parents at Harry's Food Market, located on Market Street, in Paterson, New Jersey, across from Paterson General Hospital.

Her parents were very welcoming and thankful for the fruit basket. I was introduced to Mary's aunts, uncles, and cousins. We had dessert and stimulating conversations. I was even invited to go fishing with her father in their personal pond located on their property. He stated he had stocked bass in the pond many years ago, and many of them now weigh over eight pounds. I stayed for over two hours, and then I followed Mary back to campus.

One Sunday morning, while attending St. John's The Evangelist Church, a Catholic church located on Massachusetts Avenue, a good walking distance from campus, I saw Mary sitting several pews ahead.

After the service was completed, I greeted her and told her I was not aware that she attended St. John's. She responded she would come here on occasions, and also attend other Catholic churches in the area.

I asked her if she had walked, and she responded it was too far. After I told her I had walked, she asked me if I wanted to ride back with her. I told her I would. On the way back she asked me if I had eaten breakfast. After I told her I did not, she asked me if I wanted to go to her favorite breakfast place.

At the restaurant, I don't know what came over me, but I asked her if she would like to go with me to my brother's wedding. Up to that point I had not made up my mind if I wanted to go alone or take someone. Was that my heart speaking for me? I did ask her, and I clearly heard my words. While I was reflecting on what I had just said, Mary's answer was, "Are you asking me out to a date?"

I thought to myself, I didn't think of it before as being a date, but it is. Now what do I say? Again, while I was thinking how to respond, my mouth blurted out, "Yes". Her response was, "Of course, just let me know the date."

I told her it was Saturday, June 21, and that I could pick her up at her house Friday afternoon, she could stay at our house with my family, and I could take her home on Sunday.

Her next question was, "Where will I sleep, do you have a guest room?" I told her we do not, but she could stay in my room. Her next question was, 'Where will you sleep?" I told her I would sleep in my brother's room. She agreed and had a big smile on her face.

I could only guess what her smile meant; was it because she considered it was to be a date, or was it because she wanted to go to the wedding? I was hoping it was the latter.

Stephanie remained a part of my life; when I would look at her picture on the top of my dresser I would think of her, and on some occasions my eyes would tear. When I listened to the radio, and heard one of the songs we would dance to, my eyes would again tear.

However, when I was in the company of others, especially Mary, I would not think of her as often. Recently, I had started to think of Stephanie when Mary came around. I asked myself, "Why is this happening?" I also felt that I was treating Mary differently. I could not pinpoint how, or in what areas, but I felt a change in me.

Prior to the school year ending, Mary and I had made tentative arrangements for me to pick her up for the wedding.

The school year ended and I spoke to her on the telephone to confirm our arrangements. She was making this a very big occasion, and described to me the dress and shoes she had purchased. She could not wait for the special occasion.

Her only concern was her hair. Her dilemma was should she have it done by her hairstylist, have it done by a hairstylist in New Jersey, or do it herself? I could not help her in that area, but I asked her who styled her hair for school events. Her reply was she did it herself. I told her, "If that's the case, you should do it yourself, because for special school events your hair was always outstanding." Her response was, "Oh, you noticed."

I had earlier informed Manny, Gladys, and Mom I had asked Mary to attend the wedding, and that she would be staying at our house. They could not wait to meet her.

I picked up Mary on Friday around noon time, and had lunch at her parent's home. That evening Jay and I made plans to dine together and have the girls meet, so they could feel comfortable and have someone to talk to at the wedding.

Mary and I arrived at my house around 5:00 P.M. Manny, Mom and Gladys were there to greet us. Mom and Gladys each gave Mary a big hug and welcomed her. Gladys gave me secret thumbs up when Mary wasn't looking. Manny politely said hello and gave me a silent "she's gorgeous."

Mary freshened up and we left to meet Jay and Ann. We met at the Madison Plaza Diner, located at Madison Avenue and Getty Avenue in Paterson, New Jersey. Jay and I had eaten there before, and Jay's father was friends with the owner. Jay's father was very likeable and was friendly with many business owners in Paterson.

Jay, who is very bold and usually states what's on his mind, blurted out to me, "Man, Tony you didn't tell me she was so beautiful." I just looked at Jay and shook my head.

Ann and Mary got along very well; I could tell by their conversation they liked each other. We had a nice dinner and went home.

We arose early in the morning, and had a quick breakfast. Mary became like part of the family and went with Mom to Gladys's house to dress, help Gladys get dressed, and do what women do just before a wedding.

The male members of the wedding party met at our house. Manny told the other guys, "Wait till you see Tony's new girl. She's a real knockout." I didn't respond.

The wedding was set to begin at 2 PM, and was a High Mass at St. Joseph's Church, the church where Gladys's family and our family would attend Sunday Mass. It was next to the school where Stephanie graduated from; the school where Stephanie and I would attend the CYO dances, the place where we would dance all night.

The wedding was superb, no one made a mistake, and Gladys looked like a princess. After the ceremony we went to Garret Mountain for photographs. The wedding reception was held at the Casino De Charles located on Union Avenue in Totowa, New Jersey.

Mary sat with Jay and Ann, and I sat at the head table. On my first visit to the table where Mary was seated, Jay blurted out, "Tony, I think Mary is just as beautiful as Steph." He caught himself and did not finish the rest of Stephanie's name. Mary looked at Jay and had a slight smile on her face. I then took a good hard look at Mary. I had never before looked at her this way. I suddenly realized she was more beautiful than I had imagined.

I then thought of Stephanie and my eyes began to tear. I quickly excused myself and went to the men's room to recoup. Jay detected something and followed me to the men's room. I asked Jay if he really thought Mary was as good looking as Stephanie. His response was, "You know I wouldn't lie to you."

His next question was, "Are you two dating?" I quickly reminded Jay of my vow. Jay said, "You're nuts, you are going to lose her." I told him, "She is not mine to lose."

Jay and I returned to the table. Mary turned to me and said, "Tony I saw all your trophies in your room, I didn't know you studied self-defense. How long have you been studying?" I told her I started studying it my sophomore year in high school. Jay said. "I have seen Tony in several competitions, and he is not the same nice Tony when he is competing."

Mary asked, "What kind of self-defense are you studying?" I told her it was Amdofudushiemro, and it means American way of self-defense. It is a composite of the most effective self-defense techniques taken from other disciplines, such as Judo, Karate, Jujitsu, Nejitsu, Savate and others.

Mary asked if I had ever used it to defend myself. I told her I only study self-defense because my grandfather once told me *a person had to be well balanced in life. Do a little of this, and a little of that. In other words, sleep well, eat well, learn well and exercise well.* So, I learned self-defense to keep myself in physically good shape, and at the same time learn the art of self-defense.

My grandfather also told me *avoid fighting at all cost, fighting should be a last resort after all other means have been exhausted.* So, to answer your question I have never used it to defend myself. I have *used other means in the past to avoid confrontations. Means such as respecting others, I try not to hurt others' feelings, and being fair, just and honest.*

Jay then said, "You ought to see what else Tony can do." My very bold friend Jay somehow got up to the microphone and made an unscheduled announcement. He said, "Ladies and gentlemen, at this time I'd like to introduce you to a special guest singer. Someone whom all of you know very well, but never heard him sing before." I immediately turned red, and said to myself I hope he isn't referring to me.

At the instant he said, "Tony Herera," I wanted to choke him. What has he done? I looked at my mom, and she smiled. She and Manny had heard me sing in the shower numerous times, and they always commented on how wonderful my singing was.

Jay knew I could sing because we sang together in the men's room at St. Joseph's CYO, but we stopped singing after high school. Besides I never sang in public, especially here in front of my family and friends.

People began to applaud and I heard several positive comments which encouraged me. I also did not want to disappoint the newlyweds, so I stood up and said a quick Hail Mary as I walked toward the microphone.

The band leader asked me what I wanted to sing. I chose something short, something easy to sing, a song I knew all the words to, and one I sang often in the shower. I told him "Night" by Jackie Wilson.

The song went over well, and I received a good reception from the crowd. As I passed Mom, she said, "That was wonderful Tony." Manny yelled, "Nice going Tony, thanks." I returned to the table and asked Jay if he wanted to sing a tune with me. I was only kidding, and I knew Jay's answer would be no. Jay's response was, "No thanks Tony. I think the audience has had enough for one evening."

Mary said, "Tony, you are just full of surprises." I asked her if she wanted to dance; they were playing a song Stephanie and I would dance to. As we danced, Mary reminded me of Stephanie. She had the same fragrance, and we danced the same way. I got caught up in her memory that I held Mary tightly, kissed her on the cheek and said, "Stephanie I love you."

At that instant Mary stopped dancing and quickly ran to the ladies room. I thought to myself, "What have I done?" Mary was in the ladies room for a long time. Ann suspected something was wrong, so she went to the ladies room to look for Mary.

They both returned several minutes later, and Mary was not the same. After the festivities were over, I took her to my house and she requested that I take her home early in the morning.

The next morning we departed for Mary's house early in the morning, as she had requested. We didn't say much to each other, and I wanted to wait until after breakfast before I apologized to her.

Once we began our journey I said to her, "Mary I want to apologize to you for last evening. I didn't want to hurt you, and I..." Mary interrupted and said, "Tony I was wrong. I love you very much, and I thought perhaps you loved me. I was also hoping I could change your mind about that vow you made to yourself. Obviously, I was wrong. I have made a big mistake and I paid for my mistake by receiving a broken heart. Tony, last night you broke my heart." I said to her, "Mary I didn't want to hurt you, I didn't want to break your heart. I am very sorry." Mary again interrupted me and said, "Tony, you must have loved her very much."

The remainder of the trip we remained silent. I dropped her at her house and I left for home.

I arrived at home and immediately Mom said, "Tony what happened to Mary?" I asked her what she meant. Mom replied, "When she first came here she was very happy, and when she left she appeared to be very upset." I said, "Mary was in love with me, and thought I loved her. She was hoping to change my mind about the vow I made." Mom's response was, "I knew she was in love you, it was written all over her face, couldn't you see that?"

Mom then asked me, "So, what happened?" I told her that when we were dancing I said, "Stephanie I love you." Mom, with a sad voice said, "Tony you broke the poor girl's heart, what is the matter with you, you know better than that." I said, "I didn't mean to."

Mom did not stop there she asked me, "Tony do you love her?" I said, "I don't know." Mom told me, "Tony you do love her. I can see that, the problem is you are preventing yourself from wanting to love her, only because of the vow you made."

Mom liked Mary, I saw that when Mary first walked into our house. Mom also knew the pain of a broken heart. She experienced that when dad died. She asked me if I had apologized to Mary. I told her of the conversation Mary and I had on our trip to her house.

That night Mary cried herself to sleep. All her hopes and her dreams were shattered. The next morning her mother saw the swollen eyes, and asked her what had happened. Mary told her what had happened, and concluded by telling her mother, "Mom I love him very much, and I was so sure he loved me."

I met with Jay during the week and he asked me what had happened to Mary. I explained the whole story to him, and his response was, "I think you lost her." I again told him, "Mary wasn't mine to lose."

I also asked him why he got me to sing at my brother's wedding, and his respond was, "Tony, you do have a wonderful voice, and I wanted you to share that with others. Besides, I think at your brother's wedding was the appropriate time."

Several weeks later Manny and Gladys came to visit. They had gone to Niagara Falls for their honeymoon. We talked about their wedding, the reception and their new apartment.   Manny asked me how Mary was, and before I could respond, Mom told them how I, because of my vow had broken her heart. Manny said to me, "Tony, your vow is now starting to affect other people; perhaps you should change your mind about it." I then left to meet with Jay.

Mom told Manny and Gladys, "I am starting to worry about Tony and that vow he made. It has been about two years since Stephanie died and he is still in love with her. He should be over it by now, and it's affecting his life and now the lives of others. He has to move on with his life." Manny stated, "I thought, when I saw Mary, she might be the one that could change his mind. Mom, you have to talk to him." Mom's reply was, "Once I know what I want to say I will talk with him, meanwhile I will pray very hard for him."

Jay and I again started our swimming ventures at Fairlawn Bathing Beach. We also began to sing together, like the old times. When we needed cash we helped his father, who always had something for us to do.

Jay and I would be runners, and deliver documents throughout New York City to his father's clients.

One evening, a week before I was to return to school, shortly after I fell asleep I had a dream. The dream seemed very real. So real, I realized it was only a dream when I woke up.

In my dream Stephanie told me, "Tony, when you drove me to school at Mount Saint Mary College, I told you that you were the only one in my life, and if anything should happen to you I would not marry. Your response to me was that you felt the same way, but regardless of what happens, the most important thing is that you wanted me to be happy. That is also what I want for you."

Stephanie continued to say, "Tony what I want for you is what you told me, to be happy. You can't be happy by continuing to love me. You can only be very happy with Mary, she loves you very much. Do not be afraid to love her."

When I woke up I was soaked and my eyes were tearing. I dressed and entered into the kitchen. Mom was awake and was drinking her very usual strong Spanish coffee. I told her of my dream. She seemed very relieved and told me she wanted to talk to me about the same subject.

Mom asked me what I thought about my dream. I responded, "I am not sure, I have to think about it." Mom quickly replied, "Tony, down deep inside you are in love with Mary, and the vow you made is stopping you from allowing that relationship to build. The only way for you to move on with your life was for you to get permission from Stephanie. That is exactly what has happened."

I told Mom, "You are right, I do love Mary and my vow was the stumbling block. I didn't want to go back on my word. I also felt I would be hurting Stephanie by destroying that special relationship we once had." Mom continued, "Tony you are a man with very strong commitments, once you make a commitment you try to stand by it. *It's okay to change your mind. That is what Stephanie wants for you.*" I thanked Mom and told her, "I think you are right, I feel a little bit better already, I will call Mary and talk to her."

Mom suggested, "Love is a very delicate subject, especially after what Mary has gone through. *I suggest you talk to her in person, so she could look into your eyes and see your sincerity.*"

I agreed. I said to myself, somehow I know that deep inside of me is a strong love for Mary, a love I was suppressing. I also know that the right thing for me to do was to love her. From now on I will try to let myself love her, just like the kind of love I had for Stephanie.

CHAPTER SEVEN

"What Do I Do Now?"

On my trip back to school, I could not get Mary off my mind. I could hardly wait to talk to her. Whatever I would say to her had to be just the right words, and my presentation had to be sincere and from the heart.

I so wanted to make up for the pain I had caused her. My only hope was that she would accept my apologies, and be able to trust me and believe that I truly love her. I also hoped that she could love me the way she did before I hurt her.

I had a big task ahead of me, but I was sure that whatever I would say to her would come from my heart. I practiced various approaches and wasn't sure which one I would use. Perhaps in seeing her something grand might come to mind.

I immediately went to my dorm. Ray had already arrived. My first question to him was did he see Mary. Ray responded that he had not seen her, but has heard that Mary was dating Joe.

My heart sank, I was devastated. I felt as though someone had stabbed me in my heart. I never counted on her dating someone else. How could this happen so quickly. I turned my head away from Ray to hide the sorrow I might portray. I told Ray I was going for a walk. I needed time to think.

It was time for me to evaluate my life. It seems I only do this when I am having difficulties. As I walked I said, "Lord, what happened here, couldn't

You help me just a little bit?" I felt as if I had lost everything. What do I do now? How could I face Mary?

I had it coming. I was told by my grandfather and many others, *"When a good opportunity arises, take advantage of it, don't procrastinate. The opportunity may never be there again."* I really blew this one. Now I know how Mary felt when I broke her heart. To me it feels like losing Stephanie all over again.

I thought of my grandfather who told me, *"There are positive sides to most situations."* The positive sides are for Mary and Joe, not for me. There is nothing but negatives for me, and many more negatives to come.

I have to change my life. I can't continue in the study group, simply because they are both in it, and it would hurt me to see them together. Perhaps I should transfer to another school?

I walked for a long time and eventually I began to think clearly. It finally dawned on me I did this to myself. I wallowed in my sorrow over losing Stephanie. I made a useless vow, and I threw Mary's love away. Now I am getting what I deserve.

So, what do I do? I can't and will not interfere with Mary and Joe's relationship. I thought of one of my grandfather's quotes, *"You cannot run away from your problems. If you run, they will be there when you stop running. You have to face them and deal with them as best as you can."* So, I will not transfer to another school, and I will remain in my study group. Also, I will not tell Mary how I feel about her. Perhaps with time my love for her will wear off, meanwhile, I will face the pain and sorrow.

Grandfather also told me, *"It will be facing your pain, your sorrow and your suffering which will make you a better person."*

I composed myself and returned to my dorm late. Time had passed so quickly that I had forgotten to eat dinner.

I had heard from other students that during the summer Joe had contacted Mary and they began seeing each other. This is how their relationship started. His timing was perfect, as though it was meant to be.

The first time I saw Mary was in our study group. I said hello, and asked her how her summer was. She responded it was fine. I could not look at her very long because my heart would throb. This is part of the pain and sorrow I said to myself I would have to endure. I was hoping it wasn't the same for her. I would not like to see her suffer.

Mary and I spoke to each other as little as possible. I found out from Joe that Mary started taking up self-defense in the nearby area. I asked her, prior to one of our study group sessions, what got her interested in self-defense. She replied, "You did, I want to stay fit and be well balanced in my life."

Ray, I, and the other study group members would continue going to social events together. Mary came on a few occasions, and when she did she would come with Joe. During Joe's basketball games she would sit with her girlfriends.

I sensed Joe was somehow acting differently towards me. It began after he started dating Mary. Perhaps he thought she and I dated, or maybe because she came to my brother's wedding, or maybe he was told how Mary once felt about me. I wasn't sure but I knew our relationship was different. My feelings for him had not changed. I treated him with kindness, respect and continued to help him with his studies. He needed all the help he could get. Mary's help was limited only because she was not in any of his classes.

One day, just before the beginning of our study session, Mary asked the group, "I just want to get a male's view point on a subject. What do you think are the three most important factors that could damage a relationship?" I mentioned trust, Ray mentioned unfaithfulness, and Jimmy stated jealousy.

Mary thanked us and stated she was getting information for her cousin, who was writing a high school newspaper article, and had asked her for some tips.

I thought about the three responses, and said to myself I sincerely kept all three in my relationships when I dated Stephanie, along with numerous others.

On my first semester break I went home and told Mom what had happened between Mary and Me. I did not want to tell her over the telephone because I knew she would be saddened and worry. Mom's response was, "Tony, everything happens for a reason. Maybe this is a good thing for all of you. Perhaps you will find someone else."

She asked me how I felt. I told her, "I feel the same way I did when I lost Stephanie." Mom quickly asked, "Did you make another vow?" I told her, "I did not, but I am still hurting inside." Mom's advice was, "Stay focused on your studies, keep busy, and maintain a positive attitude. *A heartbreak is similar to holding bitterness, anger and hatred within. It only eats away at you. Deal with it slowly* I am sure something wonderful will come your way. You are a good person, and God will take care of you."

Mom asked, "Have you told Mary about the way you feel about her?" I told her, "I found out she was dating Joe before I got a chance to tell her. I did not tell her because I do not want to interfere with their relationship."

Mom replied, "Tony, you are a good and very thoughtful person. I am sure God will send you somebody just as wonderful as Mary. *Remember good things come to those who wait.*"

Junior year was my worst year simply because of what happened between Mary and me. I was hurting inside and this hurt affected my grades. I had received my first two Bs, but I was still hopeful as I reflected on Mom's words, that something good was coming my way.

That summer was the last summer before graduation. Jay and I spent most of our time working for his father. I tried to earn as much money as possible, so I could use it to make my last year at school enjoyable.

I had told Jay of what had happened between Mary and me. Jay was very understanding and did not say I told you so. He was encouraging and told me that I would bounce back. He also told me that if he could do anything for me to just ask. I knew he was a good friend and that he meant what he had said.

During my free time I would exercise, practice my techniques, and go to the summing pool with Jay. Ann would join us when she wasn't working. They were already starting to make arrangements for their wedding, even though Jay had not proposed to her.

I couldn't wait to see where they would have their wedding. Would it be at the temple or at the church? Who would call the shots here? Jay did mention that his brother Tony would be their best man. Jay was the only child and would often introduce me as his brother Tony, even though we look very different from each other. However, both families treated the other as family.

Summer ended quickly and I had mixed emotions how I felt regarding school. On one hand I was glad to get back, finish my studies, graduate and get on with my life. On the other hand I knew I would once again experience that pain in my heart upon seeing Mary. I arrived at the school, and upon entering into my dorm room I was greeted by Ray, Mary and Joe. Mary seemed friendly, but it appeared to me that Joe had that same attitude towards me that I felt last semester.

After Mary and Joe left, I asked Ray if he detected something in Joe's attitude towards me. Ray said he did, and it is because Joe is a very jealous person. Ray further mentioned that Joe is well aware that Mary had strong feelings towards you, and he may be concerned about losing her.

I asked Ray if he knew if Mary was aware of this, and how she felt about it. Ray told me that Mary had spoken to him earlier, and asked me to tell you in confidence, that she is aware the way Joe was behaving towards you last semester. She has spoken to him and has assured him that she loves him and only him. She further mentioned she is working on trying to help Joe deal with his jealousies.

Joe, Ray, and I were in the electromagnetic application course together. I found the course to be enjoyable and fully understood the concepts and their applications. Ray found the course to be somewhat challenging. Joe was having difficulties and was barely passing the course.

I offered Joe help during our study group sessions, and he coldly replied he would manage.

Thanksgiving break came and went. Ray, James and I stayed on campus and ate at one of the local restaurants. While dining, Ray told us that Mary and Joe would not be eating with us, because Mary had invited Joe to her parents' home for Thanksgiving dinner.

Several days later, one of Mary's girlfriends told James that Joe was unable to eat Thanksgiving dinner at Mary's house, because he had to attend basketball practice. Mary had found out that basketball practice had been cancelled for the Thanksgiving break. Mary, knowing that practice had been cancelled, asked Joe how basketball practice went, and Joe told her it was very productive. Mary told Joe she was aware that practice had been cancelled, and sternly told him that she did not like being lied to, and warned him never to lie to her again. No one knew where Joe had been during Thanksgiving break.

When I heard about Mary and Joe's argument, my heart began to pounce with excitement. I thought perhaps they will break up, and if I could get her to rekindle her love for me, I thought to myself this might be the chance I was waiting for.

The first half of the final senior year ended, and everyone had received the grades they were expecting. Joe, to his surprise, passed his electromagnetic application course.

I went home for the Christmas break, and it was a joyous time for everyone except for me. I still had Mary on my mind. I often thought of what a fool I was to let her slip by. I learned as a young boy from my grandfather to *always have hope.*

My two possibilities of hope are that I would meet someone I could really love and she would love me equally, or maybe Mary would break up with Joe and fly back into my arms. I preferred the latter of the two, but I knew it was a very slim chance.

The best news during the Christmas season was that Jay asked Ann to marry him. It was interesting that Jay asked for her hand in marriage during the Christmas season, especially he being Jewish. I knew then that Ann's faith prevailed over Jay's. The same old question popped into my head. Where would the wedding be?

Jay asked Ann to marry him while the two families were dining at Ann's house on Christmas Day. I got there too late to see him pop the question. The ring was beautiful and the wedding would be in June. The exact day would be determined when they were able to get the Bow and Arrow Restaurant located in West Orange, N.J. for their reception.

Jay did ask me to be his best man. I told him I would be, but he first had to tell me if I had to wear my confirmation suit or a beanie. Jay knew exactly what I was talking about. He told me to wear my confirmation suit because the wedding would be at St. Joseph's Church. He also did mention that his Rabbi would be present to give them his blessing.

The last semester prior to graduation was just about to get under way. I arrived a day early to get a jump on things. The first bad news I heard was that over the Christmas holidays, Joe and Mary had been engaged.

Ray was the bearer of this bad news. He told me he had met Mary at the bookstore and she showed him her engagement ring. The hope I had of her breaking up with Joe just ended. I felt that agony in the pit of my stomach rekindling.

Mom did tell me that something good was coming my way. I sure hope so, but I do feel it is not going to be soon. I was told that the most difficult course for this semester was microelectronic devices and circuits. It so happened that Ray, Joe and I were in the same class.

The first day of class, I approached Joe and congratulated him on his engagement. He smiled and thanked me. Maybe his engagement to Mary gave him a sense of security, and I was no longer a threat to their relationship.

I liked Joe, but I felt Mary and I were more suited for each other. I knew I could make Mary happier than Joe or anyone else. However, that was not meant to be.

I was wrong about Joe. His engagement did not change him. He continued to treat me exactly as he had last semester.

I had seen Mary several times at the study group sessions. My feeling towards her was the same. Each time I saw her, my heart would palpitate a little faster, which would send chills up and down my body.

One study group session I was delayed because our previous instructor had detained the class. All were gathered and were waiting for me, as I entered Joe yells out, "Hey Poncho, what are you on Spic time?" I was very embarrassed and I could feel my face turn red. Mary yelled out, "Joe, what's the matter with you?" Joe walked out of the room, and Mary walked out after him.

James immediately makes a motion to have Joe expelled from the study group for unprofessional conduct. Ray agrees. I told them that the punishment was too severe and that Joe needed the study group more than any other member. I was out-voted. James was selected to be the one to tell Joe the bad news.

Mary returned alone some time later, and Ray made her aware that Joe was ousted from the group. Mary asked if that decision was Tony's idea, and she was told that I was the only one who voted in Joe's favor.

After class Mary apologized to me for Joe's behavior. Mary also stated that it was a shame that Joe was ousted from the group because he desperately depended on it to help him pass his courses.

A week later James told me that Mary and Joe had broken their engagement. I asked him what happened and he told me that Mary had told Joe to apologize to you, and maybe the study group might let him back in. Joe agreed, and told her he would go and see you, and apologize to you that evening.

The next morning Joe told Mary he had apologized to you and that everything was okay. That afternoon Ray, who knew Joe was failing the microelectronic devices and circuits course, talked with Joe and recommended he apologize to you, and afterwards he would tell the study group members of Joe's good intentions. Maybe then the group members would allow him to return to the study group. Ray assured Joe he would vote for his return.

Joe asked Ray, "Didn't you vote to kick me out in the first place?" Ray responded he did. Joe asked him what changed his mind. Ray told him, because Tony voted to keep you in, he saw something in you and believed you deserved another chance. Since then I have changed my mind.

Joe became very upset and told Ray he didn't need pity, and had no intentions of ever apologizing to Tony, nor was he interested in returning to the study group.

Mary met with James and Ray that evening and spoke to them about letting Joe back into the study group. She told them that Joe had apologized to Tony and that all was well between them.

Ray told Mary about his meeting with Joe, and that Joe had not apologized to Tony and had no intention of returning to the study group.

Mary then confronted Joe, and learned from him he had not apologized to you. Mary told him she had warned him the last time he had lied to her to never lie to her again. She also told him he could not be trusted, and that no one knows where he went Thanksgiving Day. She began to cry and gave him his ring back.

I had mixed feeling about their breakup. I felt glad in a way. Maybe this situation might be the opportunity I was waiting for. On the other hand, I did not know how Mary really felt about Joe, or how she felt about me.

Was their breakup temporary? How did she feel about me? I thought I would let things settle, see what happens, and then tell Mary how I feel about her. I also did not want to wait too long, I knew an opportunity like this might never come again.

Joe, for some reason, never apologized to Mary, and was not very upset over their breakup. I had a feeling he wasn't ready for a permanent commitment with Mary. Three weeks passed and I had an opportunity to be alone with Mary. I approached her and told her I was sorry to hear about what had happened between her and Joe. I asked her how she was feeling. She replied she was getting along.

I asked her if she thought about getting back with Joe, and her response was she wasn't sure. I was very frank with her and told her, "I made a very big mistake by making that vow to Stephanie. I want to let you know that I have loved you for a long time, and it was my vow that was preventing me from loving you. It was my stubbornness and commitment to my vow which hurt you. I am very sorry for all the grief I have caused you, and I want to know if you are willing to start over. Stephanie is gone from my life. I am starting anew, and I want to know if you can forgive me, and give me another chance."

Mary said, "Tony I always had a feeling you loved me, and I gave you many chances. That night at your brother's wedding you did hurt me. You broke my heart. I do want to love you, but I am afraid to get hurt again."

I told her, "Mary you are the first woman I have ever hurt, and I am truly sorry. I promise I will never hurt you again. Please give me the opportunity to try?" She did not respond. I held her hand and we walked for a long time.

Holding her hand I felt like I did when I first held Stephanie's hand. I felt a warm sensation running throughout my body. I did feel a difference, and the difference was this is a deeper and more mature feeling. My only hope was that Mary was feeling the same thing. I promised myself that if she could love me again, I would never hurt her again.

The following day I talked with Joe. I asked him if he had any intentions of making up with Mary. Joe told me he did not. I asked him why, and his response was he had a lot on his mind.

I told Joe that if Mary was willing, I would like to start dating her. Joe stated that Mary always had a thing for you, and I think that might be good for her. My curiosity was eager to find out why he would give Mary up so easily, so I asked him.

Joe again told me he had a lot on his mind, with issues that needed his immediate attention. He also apologized to me for his immature ethnic comments. He continued to tell me he was very upset with himself, and took some of his frustrations out on me. I told him if there was anything I could do to help, he could count on me.

Joe also told me he was dropping out of MIT for this semester, and had plans of returning next fall. I told him that he had a lot invested in this semester, and that often times, when one leaves it becomes very difficult to return.

I asked him how his grades were and he told me that his grades were part of his problem. I asked him which classes, and he responded the two classes we were both in. I told Joe I was willing to tutor him in both classes. Joe thanked me and told me he would get back to me after he made up his mind.

We departed company, and I thought to myself, Joe must have some serious problems if he is ready to give up school, and also give up Mary so easily. Did he really love her? What were his personal problems? Whatever they were, they had to be serious. I figure if he doesn't want to talk about them they must be serious.

I met with Mary and told her, "I have spoken with Joe, and I asked him if he had any objection to me dating you, that is if you want to go out with me. Joe said he had no objections." I also told her, "Joe also told me he had some personal problems he had to work out."

Mary responded, "If you want to go out with me you should ask me, not Joe." I told her she was right, but I like Joe and I do not want to interfere in your and his relationship. Mary shook her head, but did not give me any indication she wanted to go out with me.

I did invite her to attend church with me on Sunday, and afterwards we could visit her favorite restaurant. Mary's response was that she would get back to me with her decision.

Sunday came, and I had not received a response from Mary, so I assumed she was not going with me. I walked several blocks and she appeared out of nowhere. She asked me if I would mind if she walked with me. I told her it would be my pleasure. I asked her where she was going, and she responded, to church. I told her, that's interesting, so am I.

After Mass I did not assume anything, so I asked Mary if she wanted to go to her favorite restaurant for breakfast. Her answer was, "Are you treating"? My response was, "It will be my pleasure."

At the restaurant I told Mary that Jay and Ann were getting married this June, and I was asked to be their Best Man. Mary looked into my eyes and said the last time we were in here, I believe it was last April, you asked me to attend your brother's wedding. That wedding turned out to be one of the worst days of my life. Are you going to ask me to attend Jay and Ann's wedding, and is history going to repeat itself?

I told her, "I am asking you if you would like to attend my friend's wedding with me, I guarantee that this affair will be one of the most memorable activities that you will ever attend." Mary said, "In that case it will be my pleasure to attend such a festivity with you."

The next day Joe approached me and asked me if I had some spare time to talk. After my "yes" response, Joe told me he was dating a girl he loved very much. He started dating her his sophomore year of high school. This past summer they had a fight which resulted in the breaking up of their relationship. That's when he started dating Mary. Mary was just his response to his broken heart.

This past Thanksgiving, he went home and tried to restore their relationship, but she refused. That's when he decided to get engaged to Mary. He stated he only did it to get back at his old girlfriend.

This past January he received a telephone call from his old girlfriend, in which she asked to him to meet with her. He went home for the weekend and they made up. He received a telephone call from her a week ago, and she told him she was three months pregnant.

I asked Joe if he was sure it was his baby, and Joe's responded he was absolutely sure. Joe then proceeded to say he loves her very much and is leaving school to marry her.

My next question to Joe was does anyone know about her pregnancy? Joe said she is afraid to tell her parents, and I have not yet told mine.

I asked Joe how his parents felt about his girlfriend, and he said they love her very much. I asked him how her parents felt about her. Joe responded they love her, but she feels when they find out she is pregnant, they will throw her out of their house.

My recommendation to Joe was for him to tell his parents of her condition and ask them if she could move in with them. If they agree, then they could get married at their leisure. The best thing is to marry after graduation. I reminded Joe graduation was only seven weeks away.

Joe's next dilemma was his grades. He was failing two courses. He was told by both instructors that he needed an A in his finals to obtain a C grade in each course. I told Joe we have to work hard at those two courses, but I feel you can do it. Joe said he would get back to me.

Several days later Joe told me that his girlfriend had spoken to her parents, and their response was she could remain at home with them until they decided what they wanted to do. They did recommend that Joe finish school first. Joe's parents told him they would stand behind him in whatever decision he made.

I started Joe on a grueling study program, and he worked very hard at it because he had the desire he needed. I knew he was thankful, because he told Mary, "I don't know if you and Tony are dating, but if you are you're a very lucky girl."

I spent time with Mary, but it was always a getting to know each other type of relationship. She was being very cautious of our relationship, and I felt it was so because she did not want to be hurt again. I knew I had to prove to her that my love for her was sincere. I could not wait until our lips would meet. I did not want to be pushy so I was leaving that up to her.

Mary's parents were informed that she and I were now dating, and her mom's response was, "It's about time". I told Mom about it and she was elated, she said, "Tony, I told you that good things come to those who wait."

Graduation was on Friday, Mary and I made arrangements that her family and my family would sit together at our graduation. They seemed to get along very well, and according to Manny and Gladys, they said they all had a blast.

Joe did get two As on his final exams in the courses he was failing, and graduated with our class. His wedding was set for some time in late June.

Many class graduates and their families went to the same restaurant for dinner, so it was like a small graduation party. Mary's family and my family both had our graduation parties on Saturday, so we could not attend the other's party.

Two weeks after graduation I visited Mary at her home on a Sunday. I arrived early in the morning and was able to attend Mass with her and her family. Afterwards, we had breakfast at her house. Her father, a very intelligent and dignified gentleman, asked me if I wanted some free lessons on the art of fishing. I was prepared and had brought my fishing equipment. I had been fishing for many years, but I was always willing to learn some new tips.

Her Father indeed loved fishing, and was a master at it. He did outfish me, and in his humbleness he stated he had the advantage, a home court advantage.

While fishing I asked her father if it would be okay for Mary to stay at my parents' house three days to attend my best friend's wedding. His response was it is perfectly okay with me, but you have to ask Mary if it's okay with her. I smiled and thanked him.

After fishing, Mary and I went for a long walk. I told her that I missed her, she smiled. I asked her if she missed me, and she just smiled.

I asked her if she wanted to stay at my house for three days to attend Jay's wedding. She asked why three days? I told her that on Thursday evening we would attend Jay and Ann's rehearsal dinner. I told her they asked me to invite you. On Friday, Mom wants you to dine with us, and Saturday is the wedding.

Mary agreed. I told her I would pick her up early Thursday morning. I also told her I had asked her Father if it was okay with him for you to stay with us. She smiled and said, let me tell you what he said. He said, "Why don't you ask her." My response was you two have a great relationship and you know each other well.

Mary asked me, "Why didn't you ask my mom?" I told her, "The last time you stayed at my house, I asked your mom. She told me you and she had talked about it. So, I figured this time I would ask your dad."

Mary asked me, "Tony, what was it that made you change your mind about your vow?" I told her about my dream, and that my family and friends were all against my vow from the very beginning.

Mary asked, "If Stephanie didn't give you her approval for you to date me, would you be here?" I told her, "Mary, I do not know the answer to that question, but *things do happen for a reason,* and the fact is I am here and I want to be here. That is what's important."

Giving her question more thought I told her, "Mary, in thinking over what you asked me, I feel that eventually you and I are meant to be together." Mary asked, "Why do you think that?" I told her, "I think you know the answer to that question." She said, "No I don't know, tell me?" I told her, "I will tell you when the time is right." She said, "Don't wait too long."

I asked Mary, "Did you love Joe?" Mary responded, "I thought I could love him and was willing to give him a chance, but I found out he wasn't the right person."

On the way home I thought to myself I can't wait until Mary and I get our relationship together. It seems like we always struggle to talk to each other. I believe the reason is because she is not sure of my love for her. We never came right out and said to the other, I love you, nor have our lips yet met.

The wedding was only two weeks away, but it seemed like forever. Finally, Thursday came and I picked Mary up early in the morning as planned. She had a large suitcase and a new dress in a fancy carrying case.

Mom and Mary had talked on the telephone, and they had made arrangements for Mary, Mom and Gladys to go to the hair salon early Saturday morning. They were going to the Dainty Lady Salon, located on the corners of Washington Street and Broadway in Paterson.

Thursday evening wedding rehearsal was at St. Joseph's Church at 6:30 PM. Mary and I left early, and as we approached the church Mary asked, "Did Stephanie go to this church?" I thought about her question, and I wasn't sure what she was getting at. So I told Mary, "We are early, so I am going to give you a Stephanie tour because I know you are very interested in that topic." I turned onto Market Street, and stopped in front of Eastside High School. I told her, "See that corner room on the second floor, that's where I met Stephanie for the first time. It was love at first sight."

Stephanie then disappeared from my life for several weeks, but I met her at St. Joseph's Church on Sunday morning while attending Mass. She invited me to attend Monday Night C.Y.O. at St. Joseph's School.

I went around the block and stopped my car in front of St. Joseph's School. I told Mary on the second floor of this school is where C.Y.O was held. This is the place where Stephanie and I danced all night long.

I parked my car and said to her, "Mary, the Stephanie tour is over. This is our night and I want us to enjoy it. I want us to think about each other. So before we continue, do you have any more Stephanie questions?" She smiled and thanked me for the tour.

The rehearsal went well, and the dinner was held at the Alexander Hamilton Hotel. This was the place I had my high school Ring Ceremony, and it's where I gave Stephanie my high school ring. I didn't tell Mary that information because everything was going smoothly and I wanted her to think about us.

Friday was our day. I gave Mary a tour of The Silk City and the Passaic Falls. We got a take-out order of hot dogs all the way, French fries with the chili sauce, and two cokes at Libby's and ate them in Pennington Park. At her request, I took her to Meyer Brothers and Quackenbush Department stores in downtown Paterson.

That evening we dined at my house. Manny and Gladys joined us. Mom was an excellent cook, and made her special Spanish dishes. Everyone enjoyed Mom's cooking. While dining, Manny asked if Mary and I were dating. I didn't say a word, but I looked at Manny and gave him the eye with a quick and surreptitious head shake towards Mary. Manny quickly caught on and looked at Mary. Mary responded, "Ask Tony." I wanted Mary to answer that question to get her feeling on our situation. Since she passed it to me I said, "I like to think we are, what do you say Mary?" Her answer was, "That's the way I feel."

After dinner Mom caught me on the side and asked me, "Tony, did you tell Mary how you feel about her?" I knew Mom was referring to the conversation at the dinner table. I told Mom, "I have not come right out and told her." Mom then said in a stern voice, "Tony you ought to take her in your arms, give her a nice kiss and tell her you love her." My reply was, "I intend to."

Monsignor Shanley performed the wedding ceremony and a Rabbi friend of Jay's family from Temple Emanuel gave his blessings. During the service I was unable to see Mary because she was seated too far back and one of the pillars was blocking my view.

Finally, I was able to see Mary close up at the reception. She was indeed beautiful. I got a chance to dance with her and I held her close. I did feel slightly apprehensive, sort of a shaky/nervousness. I knew she was listening very closely and her apprehension was to see what name I would call her.

After the dance I took her gently by the hand and escorted her to the outside garden area. The night was clear, and the garden area was beautiful. There was a lantern shining nearby, and the new moon provided the rest of the light. It was a magnificent night and the setting was perfect.

I stopped and held her tightly. I looked into her eyes, softly kissed her lips and told her, "Mary I love you very much." Then I softly kissed her again. I could feel her relax, as if she was melting in my arms. Her nervous tension had disappeared. She responded, "Tony I love you very much. I have always loved you."

After holding her a few minutes we walked back inside to dance. As we danced I felt a new Mary, she was happy, had a big smile, a shiny glow about her, and a nice twinkle in her eyes. She was so happy tears came from her eyes. We stopped dancing and she proceeded to the ladies room to dry her tears.

Jay, who was dancing with Ann next to us, asked me, "What did you do to her now?" I told Jay they were tears of joy. Jay responded, "Oh that's what you call them."

I danced with Mom and her first words were, "Tony you told Mary, I can see the difference in her. Now you have to take care of her and treat her gently, she is a very sensitive person." I told her, "Yes, I know."

Mary returned quickly and we sat for a while to look into each other's eyes, and gently held each other's hands. Mary asked me what I was thinking, I told her first on my mind is that this is one of the happiest days of my life. Secondly, I was thinking whether I should ask Jay to sing a solo as he asked me to sing at my brother's wedding.

I excused myself from the table, went over to Jay and I asked him if he wanted to sing a solo. His reply was, "No thank you." The way he said it I knew he was sincere. I asked him if he wanted to sing a duo, and he also responded, "No, but I will sing a duo at your wedding."

Time came for me to make a toast to the bride and groom. I stood up, held up my glass of champagne, and stated, "Ladies and gentlemen, I'd like to make a toast to two beautiful people. I had the pleasure of being present when Ann and Jay first met. It was love at first sight. They are the best of friends, they have fun together and they have matured in their love together. My prayer for them is that they continue to grow in their relationship. May God bless them and all that they do."

Mary and I attended Sunday morning services at St. James Church, Totowa, NJ. We were to leave for her home early, but Mary wanted to spend more time together. We decided to go to New York City and see the early afternoon show of the "Sound of Music." Afterwards we left for her home.

On the journey Mary asked me why I loved her. I told her, "Mary, I love your inner self, I love the way you are, your faith, your feistiness, your wit, and I feel special being around you. I also like your beauty and the way you present yourself. Basically, I don't know of anything about you I do not like."

Mary stated, "Eventually, as we get to know each other, there will come a time when you will find faults in me. What will you do then?" My response was, *"We all have faults, and we have to learn to deal with them, overlook them and help each other deal with them.* I feel that we are both mature enough to help each other with any obstacles."

I asked Mary, "Why did you ask me those questions. Is that a proposal?" Her response was, "No, I am leaving that question for you."

Jay and Ann went on a ten day honeymoon to Puerto Rico. Several days later Jay was working with his father at the family business. Jay received a big office and a very handsome salary.

Ann had graduated business school and had been working as a legal secretary for a very elite law firm. Jay's father had, on several occasions, offered Ann a position within the family business. Ann declined, and her answer was she did not want to travel to New York City.

They moved into a garden apartment in Clifton, New Jersey until they could save enough money to purchase a house. Jay's father had offered to give them a down payment for their house, but Jay responded by telling his father he would like to work on it on his own; but kept that avenue opened just in case he needed help.

Jay's father also made me an offer to work at his business. It was a good offer, but I told him I wanted to stay in the engineering field. He made me another offer, which was to work with them until I was able to find employment within my field.

I temporarily took his offer. I stayed with them for three months, just enough time to learn a little about the financial world. I learned the business from Jay, who was very good at it. He had been in the business since he was in high school. He was so good at it that his father would include him on big financial matters. Jay and his father worked well together, they were both very business-oriented and professional.

I found employment with the Bendix Corporation, which was formally Bendix Aviation Corporation, located in Morristown, New Jersey. I was a research engineer working on instrumentation that would be used on space missions. This was exactly where I wanted to be.

Mary got a job working at Naugatuck Chemical Company, located in Naugatuck Connecticut. The company was located several minutes from her home. She worked as a research chemist in the Solid Fuel Propellants section. She enjoyed her work and contributed greatly to the company.

Mary's father personally knew many of the board members of the company, and when Mary applied for the position she told her father she wanted to get this job on her own. She specifically told him not to make any phone calls on her behalf.

Mary and I would talk on the telephone daily, and would meet on weekends. She would either stay with Mom and me at our house, or I would visit and stay with her parents at her house.

Mary enjoyed coming to our house because New York City was a short distance away. New York, the play capitol of the world, had lots of things for us to do and see.

Our relationship grew. We became great friends and had lots of fun together. On occasions we would go out with Jay and Ann. Mary and Ann got along very well and became good friends.

CHAPTER EIGHT

"Good Things Do Come to Those Who Wait"

✄ During the early part of November Joe called me and asked me if I wanted to be his son's godfather. I told him I was honored and thanked him for asking me. He told me the date would be Saturday November 26, at 1:30 P.M. in St. John's Cathedral. Following the baptism, a reception would be held at La Neve's Restaurant located at 276 Belmont Avenue, Haledon, N.J. Joe also asked me to invite Mary.

Mary and I attended the baptism and afterwards went to the reception. At the reception I was able to take a better look at Joe's wife, and I recalled meeting her at a basketball game years ago. She told me she was a cheerleader and cheered for Joe at Central High School.

The baby was beautiful and looked like Joe. He weighed eight pounds, was 22 inches long at birth and had a full head of hair. They were both very happy and showed their love for Joseph Jr.

At one point, Joe and I were alone and were able to talk in private. He thanked me for all that I had done for him, and asked me, "Why did you help me out, after the way I treated you"? I told him, *I know that you are a good person, and I sense that something was troubling you. Those are the times when friends should be there for each other."* Joe responded, "Again I thank you, and I am here for you if you should ever need anything."

On the way home Mary asked me, "Is Joe the baby's father?" My reply was, "Why did you ask?" Her response was, "Figuring out the time frame, Joe would have been at school when his wife became pregnant. I am not sure, but I think that may have been around the time Joe and I had just broken up." I told her, "Yes, Joe is the baby's father," and I also told her of the conversation Joe and I had at school. Mary's response was, "I knew there was something he was hiding, and I just sensed it. Joe is a very mysterious person." I further told Mary where Joe was during his mysterious disappearance, when he broke his date with her on Thanksgiving Day.

Mary and I would take time to travel on country roads, either in Connecticut or New Jersey to enjoy the countryside. We would listen to the radio as she rested her head on my side with my arm around her. We would talk about our future, children, the type of house we would buy, our friends and family.

One evening as we were driving, Mary asked me, "Tony, why don't we go someplace quiet and make out." I told her, "I would love to very much, but I don't think that's a good idea." Mary's response was, "Whenever it comes time for us to be romantic or intimate, you shy away, why?" I told her, "I went through that with Stephanie, and things would get out of control. It so happened on one occasion I was weak and she was strong. Fortunately she said, "No!" On another occasion she was weak and I was strong. Finally we came to an understanding no temptations until we married."

I also told her, "My sister and her boyfriend once experienced a time when they were both weak and it cost her life. So let's leave the romantic stuff till after we marry. I promise you won't be sorry." Mary's response was, "Well I wasn't thinking of going that far." I said, "Neither was my sister."

Mary asked me what had happened to my sister. I told her what had happened between Lucy and John. She stated, "Oh Tony I am so sorry. Is that her picture on your living room wall between you and Manny?" I told her, "It is." She said, "She was very pretty."

I asked Mary, "If you saw the picture in the living room, why didn't you ask who she was before?" Mary said, "I thought she was your sister, and something told me not to ask at that time."

On another occasion, while we were eating in a small restaurant in Connecticut, Mary said, "When you sang at your brother's wedding, you sang Jackie Wilson's song "Night." Did you sing that song for Stephanie?" I thought for a few seconds before responding. I felt Mary was still trying to get an answer to why I had called her Stephanie. I thought of the words to the song: "Night here comes the night, another night to dream about you. Once more I feel your kisses. Once more I know what bliss is. Come back my darling you're gone, but you come back into my arms each night." The words clearly point that I was thinking about Stephanie. I truthfully responded, "Yes."

Mary then said, "Tony, that night, while we were dancing, we danced to the Platter's song "Remember When." Was that a song you and Stephanie danced to?" I said, "Mary you have a very good memory. That was indeed the song you and I danced to that night. It was also the song Stephanie and I danced to many times. That was also the last song I remember hearing when I saw Stephanie for the last time. I remember it distinctly, because after the song ended, Stephanie and I talked about the time when we first met."

Mary responded, "Oh, that's why you called me Stephanie, you were thinking about her." I said, "Yes, I was thinking about her. When I hear that song today, it reminds me of how it almost caused me to lose you. Remember it was you I kissed that night, and it was your image I had on my mind when I kiss you, but thinking of the last time I saw her it was her name I blurted out. Mary could you please put that night to rest?" Mary said, "Tony I love you."

Mary and I had been dating for over a year, and one evening, as we traveled to my house, after dining at Umberto's Restaurant in Little Italy, New York. Mary asked me, "If we get married, where will we live?" I quickly responded, "I haven't asked you yet." Mary said, "I think we should live in New Jersey. Your job is there, I can get a job anywhere, and we are close to New York. Besides, the salaries are much higher in this area."

This was the first indication Mary said anything about getting married. I am glad she mentioned it because I was thinking about the same thing. However, I had no clue on how to approach the subject. Now that I knew where she stood, it made it easier for me.

The end of the weekends were terrible because we had to say good bye. We would not see each other for an entire week. We deeply felt our love as we embraced before departing. I felt just wonderful being in her presence. We both knew if we were married, we would not have to say good bye till next weekend.

One Sunday afternoon, after Mary had departed, I said to my mother, "Mom I would like to marry Mary. What, do you think?" Mom smiled and said, "I think it's a great idea, have you asked Mary yet?" My response was, "No, I wanted to ask how you felt about it first." Mom replied, "Tony you don't need my permission, you know I love Mary like a daughter." I told Mom, "I know how you feel about her, I am thinking about leaving you alone." Mom said, "Tony, I am very capable of taking care of myself. Who was here while you were away at school, no one? So go and get married. You have my blessing."

One weekend, while I was visiting Mary, her father and I were fishing at their pond. I asked him for his permission to marry his daughter. His response was, "Tony, I knew from the day I first met you that you and Mary would one day marry. Thank you for asking me for my permission. I would love to have you in our family." I thanked him. He asked me, "Have you asked Mary yet?" I told him, "I did not, and could we keep this between ourselves until I ask her?" He agreed.

The next day I was able to be alone with Mary's mom and I asked her the same question. She hugged me, kissed me on the cheek and said. "Tony I think it's wonderful." I had her sworn to secrecy that she would not mention anything to Mary, because I had not yet asked her daughter to marry me. She agreed. I also asked her mother if she knew Mary's ring size. She quickly responded seven and one-half.

Now comes the hard part, I have to shop for an engagement ring and then ask Mary if she would marry me.

Then it hit me, what if Mary said no? I know her well enough to know her answer would be yes. However, my grandfather taught me *never to assume anything.* It would break my heart if she said no. My grandfather also taught me to think positive and move on. So, if she said no, I will cross that bridge when I get to it.

During that week Mom and I looked at engagement rings. I asked her to come with me to get a woman's opinion. I was looking at more expensive rings, but Mom suggested that even though Mary comes from a rich family, she is very conservative and does not like to flaunt things.

I finally found a one carat marquis-shaped diamond that Mom and I both liked, and it was in the middle of the road, expense-wise. I took Jay and Ann to see it and they both agreed it was something that Mary would like. So I purchased it.

Jay had asked me when the wedding would be, and I told him after I propose to Mary, we would come up with a date. I also asked Jay if he would be an usher. He knew my brother Manny would be my best man. Jay said he was waiting to be asked and responded he would.

It was again time for me to go to Mary's house for our weekend date. I asked her if she wanted to attend Mass at St. John's in Cambridge, Massachusetts near our old Alma Mater on Sunday, and afterwards visit her favorite breakfast restaurant. She replied she'd loved to, and indicated it was a long ride, so suggested we leave very early in the morning. We both agreed.

After Mass, while sitting at our favorite table at the restaurant I said to her, "Mary I love you very much and I'd like to ask you to marry me?" Mary responded, "Would you like to ask me or are you asking me?" I rephrased it by saying, "Mary, I love you very much and want to marry you, will you marry me?" Mary said, "Yes, yes, yes." I was very relieved.

I then placed the engagement ring on her finger. Mary stated, "Tony it's beautiful, I love it."

Mary said, "I knew you were going to propose to me as soon as you asked me to come here to eat." My response was, "Why did you think that?" She said, "This is the place I would have picked because this is the place you asked me for our first date, and the place where I believe we first felt close to each other."

Mary also said, "I had a feeling you were going to ask me to marry you a while ago, so I told my mother, "If Tony should ask my ring size tell him seven and a half." I told Mary, "I should have known, I thought it was odd when I asked your mom for your ring size and she immediately blurted out the size."

Mary was so happy she went around the restaurant telling everyone she had just gotten engaged, and showing them her ring. The owner and his staff came out with a cake and sang happy engagement to you.

We made arrangements to wed on May 19, 1962. Mary requested the reception be held at her backyard, which she loved. She would have it catered, set up tents and decorated the yard with many beautiful flowers, and have a five piece band.

The following weekend Mary visited our house. We had dinner on Saturday evening at Mom's house. Gladys, Manny, Jay and Ann dined with us. While dining, Mary and I broke the news that we had become engaged. Mary proudly showed everyone her engagement ring. There were many hugs, kisses and congratulations.

I asked Manny if he would be my best man and Manny responded, "For my favorite brother, I would be honored." Mary and I told them we had set a tentative date for May 19th.

Manny and Gladys told us they also had good news. The first good news was that Gladys was expecting a baby. The baby was due in six months. They even had names picked out. If it were to be a boy he would be called Joseph after Gladys' father. If it were to be a girl it would be called Lucy after Manny's and my sister.

Mom had her suspicion that Gladys was expecting, she could see it in the glow of her face, but never said a word.

Manny also told us that he was starting his own trucking company. He had the support of his current boss, who would provide Manny with some of his excess customers. He would also loan Manny some of his spare trucks until Manny's new trucks were delivered.

Manny was approved for a small business loan, and had rented a location in Secaucus, N.J. He also ordered three new trucks, and was in the process of interviewing truck drivers, some of whom owned their own trucks. Manny had obtained the necessary permits and the required insurance. His new trucking company would be called Manny's Trucking Company.

Manny had been secretly working on opening his own trucking company for one year, and had kept it silent in case it did not work out. Finally, everything fell into place for him. The right people came to his aid, the government rewarded him with a business loan, the location he wanted became available, and he had good luck in his recruiting.

Mom was suspicious that Manny was working on something, but kept it to herself. We all gave Manny a big hug and congratulated him. Jay stated, "Manny if you need any extra cash, come to the Pearlman Group, we can give you a very low interest loan, and we may be able to recommend some customers to you." Manny thanked Jay.

After dinner we all went to the movies to see Lawrence of Arabia, which was playing at the Montclair Theater.

Mary's parents invited Mom, Manny and Gladys to their home for the weekend. The idea was for everyone to get acquainted. Mary and her mom personally prepared the meals we ate. I had no idea that both of them were excellent cooks. Usually, the food cooked at her house was prepared by the housekeepers.

The weekend was very pleasant; Mom gave Mary's mom some of her Spanish recipes.

On the way home Mom told me, "Tony, I told you good things come to those who wait." Mary is smart, attractive, a very nice person, and she can even cook."

Manny's business began to pick up. He had hired three more drivers, and had purchased two additional trucks. He would provide both cross country and local deliveries. As he anticipated, his previous employer helped him out tremendously.

Gladys and Manny had their baby. It was a girl, 20 inches long and weighed 6 pounds and five ounces. They named her Lucy. She was a beautiful girl who received the best features of both Manny and Gladys. The godparents for the baptism were Mary and I.

Mary devoted her spare time planning for the wedding, calling the necessary people, picking out her wedding gown, and making arrangements with her church. I spent most of my time looking for an apartment. I finally located a two bedroom garden apartment in Parsippany, N.J. The building was new, so all that Mary and I had to do was to pick out furniture.

The apartment consisted of a small kitchen with a dining area, two bedrooms, a bathroom and a large living room. We bought most of our furniture in Robok's Furniture Store located on Market Street in Paterson. Our weekends were spent decorating the apartment. Mom, Manny, Gladys, Jay and Ann would visit and help decorate.

Mary had obtained employment at Hoffman- La Roche Inc, in Nutley, New Jersey. She made prior arrangements to start working after our return from our honeymoon.

Our wedding day was finally here, and Manny, Jay and I stayed at a very quaint bed and breakfast near Mary's house. Ann, Gladys and Mom stayed at Mary's house. There were extra bedrooms at the maid's quarters for the men to stay, but Mom suggested we stay at another location to allow the girls to dress and fuss. Mom also knew the wedding would be a lot of work for the maid and her husband, and did not want to add an extra burden on them by having guests stay with them.

The ceremony was a full Mass at St. Francis Church in Naugatuck; everything went well, and no one fainted. The weather was great and we were able to take photos at Mary's yard.

The reception setting was spectacular; the food was catered by one of Connecticut's finest restaurants, and the five piece band turned out to be an eight piece. Mary's dad and I conspired to add a piano and two violins, and they were outstanding. Everyone seemed to be enjoying themselves.

Jay came over to Mary and me and said he was ready to sing our duo as he had promised at his wedding reception. I asked Jay if he would allow me to sing a solo. I had previously talked to Jay, and we had agreed that we would not sing together, but I would sing alone.

Mary said to herself, if he sings that Jackie Wilson song he sang at his brother's wedding I am going to throw the wedding cake at him.

I got to the microphone and announced I was going to sing one of Jackie Wilson's songs. I took a long look at Mary, and I could see a very surprised look on her face. I then said, "I would like to dedicate this song to my wonderful wife. I sang Jackie Wilson's song, "Alone at Last."

After the song was over Mary thanked me and kissed me. She said, "That's why Dad asked to have the piano and the two violins, so you could sing that song". My response was, "Mary, you think too much."

That evening, after the reception, Mary and I changed our clothes and stayed at a nearby hotel. Our bags had been previously packed and we were ready to depart for San Juan early the next morning. We left after breakfast and took a late afternoon flight from Newark Airport.

We had a wonderful ten days traveling throughout the island. We ate native foods at local restaurants, and we visited some of my relatives. Our visits were very short at the relative's houses. The visits were just to introduce Mary to my family.

I thought I knew Mary, but she surprised me with how fluent she was in Spanish. I asked her why she never told me she spoke Spanish. She responded, "Let's just say, it's like the way you surprised me with the karate trophies in your bedroom, and how you also surprised me with your wonderful singing." She told me she learned her Spanish in high school.

Jay and Ann finally saved enough money to buy land, and have their house built. They bought land in a new development, located on the end of a cul-de-sac in West Essex, N.J., and a short distance from Jay's parents' home.

Jay and Ann did all the planning for their house. Jay even subcontracted most of the work. The same house, if purchased completed would have cost thousands of dollars more.

Their house was beautifully decorated; it was like entering into a show room. When Mary and I first visited their house, Mary kidding with them said, "Is it okay for me to touch anything?" Jay quickly responded, "No, you can't. You also have to stand all evening and take off your shoes." We all laughed and then Jay said, "Please relax, and make yourselves at home. Everything looks like this because it is new, so let's break it in."

Later on in the evening while we were having coffee, I overheard Mary whisper to Ann, after she had asked Mary how the honeymoon went. Mary responded, "That Tony is very romantic, I also surprised him when he learned I speak Spanish better than he."

That evening before going to bed I said to Mary, "By the way, I think my Spanish is much better than yours." Mary said, "Tony, you were listening to our conversation." I replied, "You spoke so loudly I thought you wanted the world to hear it."

Mary and I planned to save enough money to buy a house, start a family, and start our own business. I told her I was interested in starting a manufacturing company that would provide equipment and parts to our government to be use in our space program.

I told her I had received this idea from Stephanie's father. Then it dawned on me. I never was able to locate the Mullens. I wonder how they were, and how his company was doing. I also thought about the job he had offered me, and wondered if the offer was still good.

Our dilemma was, where do we start? Do we build our house first or invest our money in our dream company?

We decided it would be more prudent if we were to buy a house first. If we invested our monies in a dream (our company) and it didn't work out, we would lose everything. If we bought our house first, and afterwards invested in our dream company, and the company failed, we would still have our house.

On Sundays we would either go to Mom's house for a late Sunday afternoon lunch/dinner, or spend the weekend at Mary's. One afternoon Manny, Gladys, Baby Lucy, Mary and I were at Mom's house, and Mom announced that there was a house for sale two houses away from her house. She also stated that this was the first house for sale on this block in a very long time.

Mom was directing her words at Gladys and Manny who had announced months ago they were looking for a house in the area. Manny stated, "That house is currently under contract to Mr. and Mrs. Manuel Herera."

Everyone congratulated Manny and Gladys. Mom asked them, "Why didn't you tell me?" Manny responded, "It happened so fast we didn't get a chance." I said, "That's great now you can keep an eye on Mom." Mom said, "No, now I will be a built-in babysitter for Lucy." Mary's comment was, "This is great, when we visit, we can kill two birds with one stone."

The house was a cape with three bedrooms, very similar to Mom's house. It was a good location to raise children.

Several months later Manny and his family moved into their new house. Manny and Gladys had a house welcoming party. The guests were Mom, Mary and I, and Jay and Ann, and some of Manny and Gladys' friends.

One evening, after a very fine dinner at Mom's house, a conversation arose pertaining to child rearing, and what type of punishment should be used to discipline children. Jay's comment was a good swat on the fanny is a good way to reprimand. Ann disagreed and said a good stern talking is the way to handle it. Mary said that it depends on what they did, the severity of what they did, and if they had done it before.

Then they all turned to me, and asked, "Tony, what would your grandfather say?" All of them at one time or another heard me quote one of my grandfather's words of wisdom.

I stood up, and using a Charlie Chan voice said, "Grandfather says, first, beyond a reasonable doubt the child must be found guilty as charged. After his conviction the punishment must be swift and sure. The punishment must fit the crime, and finally the punishment must be executed by the child's parents or legal guardians." Everyone laughed.

Mom said, "Tony did you ever show Mary your grandfather's letters?" I responded, "No." I knew all were eager to find out what letters Mom was talking about, so I told them. "My mother's parents raised me for several years, while my mother was in the United States. My grandfather would always talk with me, explain things to me, teach me and show me things to help me grow up to be a better person. When I came to the U.S., my grandfather and I would write to each other. In my letters I would update him on my life, tell him of my personal experiences and any problems I was going through. He would write back and provide me with direction and words of wisdom. Many of them were sayings, expressions and teachings he had learned from past generations. I found those letters to be very helpful in my life, so I have saved all of them, and one day I plan to use them as a teaching tool for our children."

Mary said, "They sound very interesting, I am looking forward to reading them." Jay said, "I have heard Tony quote many of them, and they are very practical, interesting, and appropriate for our generation and generations to come."

That evening Mary stayed up till three o'clock in the morning reading my grandfather's letters. They were written in Spanish, so on occasion she would ask me the meaning of some words. When she was finished she told me, "Tony, these letters are wonderful, your grandfather was very special, he was full of much wisdom and he loved you very much."

Mary and I would spend our evening hours making plans for our new company. Our plan was to have our company provide equipment, parts, circuits or anything that was needed to make our space program successful.

We stayed away from providing instrumentation equipment, only because the company I was working for was already providing this type of equipment. It was also against Bendix Company policy for an employee to compete with them. Furthermore, Bendix had a government contract and was providing very good products, making it hard for others to compete with them.

We would make it a point that whatever we provided would be state of the art equipment. If it were to be circuits we would make them smaller, respond faster, withstand more heat, and last longer. At the same time we would try to keep the expense down.

In order to come up with the proper equipment we would need to do much research and have the right people involved, people capable of bringing our product to the next level. We would need experts in various fields. Mary would work with the chemical engineers, I would work with the electrical engineers and Joe had indicated he would be assisting us with the mechanical engineering aspects. Jay even volunteered to help us with the financially end. Our plans were starting to fit into place.

Mary and I kept good on our previous plans to first purchase a house prior to starting up our company. We were able to buy a four bedroom split level house in Parsippany, New Jersey, just several miles from our garden apartment. We moved in and purchased additional furniture to fill the extra rooms. One bedroom being a future bedroom for our first child, one being a guest bedroom, and the fourth bedroom would be used as our office.

Twelve months later the child's room became baby Tony's bedroom, and sometime after that our guest room became baby Lisa's room. With two small children, Mary and I were still able to save enough money to begin our dream company, The Herera Industries.

Jay and I were on the same baby schedule. He and Ann had their first child two months before we had Tony, and they had their second three months after we had Lisa. Jay's son was named John and their daughter Melissa. Mary and Ann would take the children to parks, shopping, to the zoo and numerous other fun areas.

We located and rented the building of an old smaller company which had gone out of business. The previous tenant had passed away from a heart attack and the company dissolved. The location had a very secure foundation, plenty of open area, and large entry doors in the front and rear of the building. It also had two bays for shipping and receiving. There were three offices, a larger office which could be used for administration, a smaller office for the parts department and a third office we would use as a lunch room.

The potential was here, it was a perfect set up. The building had a good heating and air conditioning system, and could house fifty employees, not counting office workers.

It was located in Fairfield, New Jersey very close to Route Number 46, and the best part was the rent fell within our budget.

We were able to get a small government contract providing switching devices, seats, safety belts, utensils and other small devices to be used by NASA. We hired fifteen employees. They were assemblers, wiremen, and mechanics. We also hired a friend of Jay's family, a John Magallon, a top notch machinist.

The new employees were all excellent workers. They enjoyed their jobs and immediately became like a family. Mary came up with the idea for us to provide similar products to the automobile industry. We did, and before long we got some contracts from major auto makers. As a result, our work force was increased.

Through the course of our research, we found out that NASA was looking for a new kind of heat system protection for the space shuttle orbiter. Previously used systems were not maneuverable and followed ballistic re-entry trajectories parachuting into a watery landing in the ocean. Their only protection during re-entry was shedding layers of heavy resinous heat shields.

We had to come up with something that would withstand temperatures well over 3,000 degrees Fahrenheit, temperatures caused by friction upon re-entry, temperatures which can melt iron, steel and chromium. They would also have to withstand temperatures as low as minus 250 degrees Fahrenheit.

We first had to come up with the type of materials to use. To be more competitive we set our goals for the material to be able to withstand temperatures well over 4,000 degrees Fahrenheit. Then we had to come up with the equipment for us to be able to test the material. Finally, we had to be able to secure the government contract. Our quest began.

One Sunday afternoon Mary and I went with the kids to visit Lucy's and my grandfather's graves. As we approached, I noticed on the both graves fresh roses laid out in the manner Stephanie had taught me.

Mary asked me about the roses and why they were laid out in that manner. I explained to her the meaning. I wondered who had placed the roses there. It could have been Manny or Mom, but I could not remember if I had ever showed them or explained to them the meaning of that particular format.

That afternoon we were having our Sunday lunch/dinner at Mom's house. While dining, I asked both Mom and Manny if they had been to visit Lucy and Grandfather's graves. They both responded they had not been there in several months.

On the way home it came to me that it must have been Stephanie's aunt, Sister Clara. It was from Sister Clara that Stephanie learned the meaning of placing the roses in that particular format. Stephanie had told me that she had brought her Aunt Clara to visit my grandfather's grave. Sister Clara told Stephanie, that in the future, when she would visit her family graves, she would also visit my grandfather's grave.

On the way home, I told Mary it must have been Stephanie's Aunt Clara, a nun, who must have placed the roses on Lucy and Grandfather's graves. I also asked Mary if she would mind if I returned to the cemetery in an attempt to get information from the cemetery's caretaker, regarding the person who had visited Lucy and Grandfather's graves.

I told Mary if I could get a license plate of the vehicle used by the person who placed the roses on the graves, whom I believe to be Sister Clara, I might be able to contact her. Then I could obtain from her the address or telephone number of the Mullens.

I asked Mary if she would have any objection of me contacting the Mullens. Mary's response was, "Tony, years ago when I had just met you, your night dreams were about Stephanie, those same years she was my nightmares. Once you put the wedding ring around my finger those nightmares have disappeared. To answer your question, I would like to meet the Mullens."

I pulled into the cemetery and caught the attendant as he was about to leave. I asked him who had visited Lucy's and my grandfather's graves.

After I pointed out the graves to him, he said he distinctly remembered because it was a nun who drove a car with New York plates. I asked him if he could, upon her next visit get her plate number for me. He was hesitant until I explained the circumstances to him. He took my name and a telephone number where I could be contacted, and advised me he would call me when he had the information.

During that week, we visited Jay and Ann. Jay and I were in the living room talking, and Ann and Mary were in the kitchen. Mary asked Ann how well she knew Stephanie. Ann responded, "We were very good friends. We were in high school for four years. In fact she was the one who introduce me to Jay."

Mary asked Ann, "Did Tony and Stephanie get along well?" Ann said, "They got along very well; they were always together and went many places." Mary asked Ann, "How did Tony get along with the Mullens?" Ann responded, "They also got along very well, why did you ask that question?" Mary told Ann, "I asked because Tony is very interested in trying to contact her parents, and I have no clue why." Ann's response was, "I think Mr. Mullen was the one who encouraged Tony to go into the engineering field. He also liked Tony very much. I even think he had offered Tony a job after graduation from college."

Mary told Ann, "Mr. Mullen even gave Tony the idea for the company we started. I think he had a big influence on Tony's life. Maybe this is why he wants to contact him."

One Saturday evening, while dining at Mary parents' home, I talked with Mary's father regarding the progress of our company, and about the bid we were about to make in an attempt to get a very large government contract, a contract which would drastically enhance our business.

Mary's father asked, "If you were to get the contract, do you think you would be able to fulfill the contract?" I asked him, "What do you mean?" He said, "Wouldn't this new contract require more manpower and a larger facility?" I said, "Yes, it does. If needed I can obtain the required manpower, and I can either move to a bigger location, or obtain another smaller location. I believe the two locations would be able to fulfill our needs. If I have to, I can also subcontract some of the work to competitors, even though this would mean a smaller profit."

Mary's father stated, "If you really want this contract and you think you can handle it, I have some friends in Washington who could provide me with information which might be very helpful to you when you submit your bid."

My response was, "No thank you sir." He said, "Tony, that is the way things work in business, you have to have an edge." I again said no and thanked him. He then stated, "Tony you have employees who have families and this contract will put food on their tables, think of them." My response was, "I know sir, but all the other bidders also have employees and they too have families, they also need food on the table, how about them? I'll just let nature take its course, and whoever should have the contract, so be it."

Mary then jumped into the conversation and said, "No thanks Dad, it's the same as when I asked you not to make any phone calls when I was applying for a job at Naugatuck Chemical Company."

Much research was conducted in an attempt to come up with the materials which would stand up to the high temperatures. We tried many combinations of reinforced carbon-carbon, inconel foil insulators, titanium, tiles, quartz blankets, resin and ablator. Finally a promising combination of resin, quartz and phenolic impregnated carbon ablator (PICA) seemed to be the best.

Mary found a company that would test our shields. It was called NASA Ames International Heating Facility located in Mountain View, California. The testing would entail placing a puck size sample in a twenty foot long hollow tube, and two charges are emitted which create a bolt of lightning (a plasma torch) directed at the sample. The lightening torch travels at the speed of seventeen thousand miles per hour and heats up to three times the temperature of the sun.

We provided a sample to NASA Ames, and the results of the test were documented, and a certified copy was given to us. The testing facility would also maintain a copy for their records and would be available for government inquiries.

Mary and I consulted with Jay, who had more insight into the financial world. After many hours of calculating we came up with a proposal and a bid. We closely followed the format provided in the application, and attached a copy of the test results.

Afterwards, Jay commented, "If I were the one making the decision I would surely award the contract to the Herrera Industries." I asked him, "Why?" Jay replied, "Tony you are providing a better product than they asked for, your heat results were incredible, and your bid, I believe is reasonable."

Our proposal was submitted, and I wasn't sure how many other companies submitted one, but I knew we were in competition with very large and well-known companies. I wondered if Mr. Mullen had submitted a proposal.

The government would have to review each application carefully, and justify why the contract should be awarded to the company it had chosen. They would also conduct background checks on the top contenders. It was a long process and would take many months.

One evening when I arrived at home, Mary told me the caretaker of the cemetery had called and left the information I requested. I looked at the paper and it was a New York license plate number.

I called the Paterson Police Department and asked the dispatcher if he could look up the plate number for me. I was told he could not provide such information. He advised me to write to Motor Vehicle and provide them with a bona fide reason why I needed the information.

I called the Paterson Police Detective Bureau and asked to speak to Detective Rogers. I was told he would be in at nine o'clock tomorrow morning.

The next morning I spoke to Detective Rogers. He informed me that motor vehicle information is not generally provided to the public, unless there is a bona fide reason. I explained to him the nature of my request. He remembered me speaking to him years ago when I asked for his help in trying to contact Mr. Mullen. I further explained it could be Stephanie's Aunt, Sister Clara.

Detective Rogers told me he would check with Motor Vehicle, and if the plate number came back to a convent, he would give me the information. If it came back to a private resident, he would be unable to give me the information. I agreed and thanked him.

Later on in the same day Detective Rogers called me and told me the license plate came back to The Graymoor Sisters located in Garrison, New York. He also gave me directions to the convent.

CHAPTER NINE

"Life is Full of Many Surprises"

✵ The first available Sunday, Mary and I took the children and went on a nice ride to Graymoor to visit Stephanie's aunt, Sister Clara.

It was a beautiful day and the children stayed outside to walk around the beautiful grounds. Mary came in and stayed at the entrance foyer to keep an eye on the children. I kept the door ajar and entered into a large visitor's area, where I was met by a joyous elderly sister.

She introduced herself as Sister Madelyn. I introduced myself and told Sister Madelyn I was here to visit Sister Clara. Sister Madelyn responded, "Perhaps you mean Sister Claire." At this point I was not sure if it was Sister Clara or Sister Claire, so I said, "Yes sister."

Sister Madelyn called for Sister Claire on a house telephone; as we waited she said to me, "We did have a Mother Superior named Clara, but that was several years ago. She has passed on."

I said to myself I am sure it was Sister Clara. If she has passed on, I will not be able to contact the Mullens. I thought I would wait for Sister Claire, and ask her if they had information regarding the Mullens.

Sister Claire walked into the room and when I saw her face my heart began to beat very hard throbs. Blood quickly rushed to my head. I got chills all over my body. I could not believe my eyes. For a second I thought it was Stephanie, and I accidentally yelled out Stephanie. It was Stephanie, and she cried out, "Tony."

Mary heard me cry out Stephanie and looked into the room. She looked at Sister Claire's face and knew it was Stephanie. She had stared at her picture on top of my dresser in my college dorm for almost four years.

Mary thought to herself, she is more beautiful than her picture. Mary turned away and walked outside. Her heart began to throb, getting progressively faster and louder. She thought to herself this is my worst nightmare. She thought her days of worrying of the relationship between Tony and Stephanie were over.

She asked herself, how could this be? Was her death a lie? Did she and Tony break up and Tony has finally found her? Mary's eyes filled with tears. She asked herself, what is going to happen now, am I going to lose him? I love him very much; he is a perfect husband, and a great father. What about our children? There were many questions on her mind and many decisions to make. She felt as though her heart was broken in two.

I ran to Stephanie and we embraced. We held each other tightly. We both had tears in our eyes. Then I said to her, "I thought you were dead." She said to me, "I thought you were dead." Stephanie, with tears running down her cheeks told me, "My father came to visit me shortly after you and my father's cousin Michael had taken his boat to Martha's Vineyard, and told me you had been killed in an automobile accident. He said your mother had taken your body to be buried in Puerto Rico next to your father. He also gave me a newspaper clipping of the accident. I have kept it all these years."

Stephanie continued, "My father also told me that my mother was very upset and was under heavy sedation. I, in trying to deal with my broken heart, and unsure of my future, could not speak to her about it for several days.

I knew there could never be anyone else in my life. During that same time, I received a call from Aunt Clara. I told Aunt Clara what happened to you, and she invited me to stay with her for a while until I could recuperate from my broken heart. I left school and stayed here at Graymoor with Aunt Clara. It was then I decided to become a nun. Aunt Clara never brought the incident up to my mother, father, nor have we ever spoken about it again.

Here is the place I could be at peace with myself. Here is where I was able to hold on to the fond memories we had. After a few weeks, I called my parents and told them where I was and of my decision to become a nun. My mother understood, but my father was against it. I told them it was my decision.

I also tried to call your mother, but she had moved and I was unable to contact her or Manny. Whenever I visited New Jersey, I would go to Lucy's and your grandfather's graves and put fresh roses on them. It was my way of remembering you. It was as though I was putting those roses on your grave."

I told Stephanie, "When I returned home from bringing your father's boat to Martha's Vineyard, your father told me you were killed in an automobile accident on campus. He told me you were buried at Holy Sepulcher Cemetery in Totowa, New Jersey. He even took me there and showed me your grave. He also told me your mother was very upset and was under a doctor's care.

I kept trying to contact your mother to give her my condolences, but your parents had moved and I was unable to contact them. I came here because someone had placed roses on my grandfather's and Lucy's graves in the same format you use. The caretaker got your plate number and here I am. I thought it might be your Aunt Clara. So I came here to see her in an attempt to contact your mother and father."

Stephanie, with more tears in her eyes said, "My father did this to us to break us up, I was fooled, I thought he liked you. How could he do this to us? He destroyed our lives."

I asked her if she was happy, and she replied, "I was until I saw you." I told her, "Your father did this because he loves you and wanted you to have a better life. He did not have any confidence in me, and thought I would not be able to provide you with the type of life he had in mind for you, so he broke us up with the idea that you might find a better life, and I think you have."

Her reply was, "He never gave me a chance to make that decision." I told her, "You have moved on with your life, and you have found something more meaningful, something more valuable than our relationship. You have found someone better than me. You have found Jesus and I believe you are living a better life."

I told Stephanie, "You have kept the vow that you made, that if anything should happen to me you would never marry. I made the same vow to myself, only I have failed." I told her about Mary and the dream I had, in which she told me to marry Mary.

Stephanie asked me, "Tony, are you happy?" I responded, "Yes I am." She replied, "That is also what I want, for you to be happy. If you are happy with Mary, then I am happy for you."

I told her, "I have some people I want you to meet. Could you please wait here for a minute while I go and get them?" As she shook her head in a yes manner, I wiped the tears from her eyes with my hankie.

I went to the car and spoke to Mary. Mary asked me, "What is going to happen to us now?" My response was what do you mean?" Mary asked, "Is that woman Stephanie?" I said, "That woman is Sister Claire, and yes that woman is also Stephanie." Mary asked, "Am I going to lose you now?" I told her, "Mary you are the only woman in my life, and I love you very much. Sister Claire's appearance is not going to change anything." Mary's response was, "Tony do you mean that?" I said, "With all of my heart."

I told her the story of what her father had done to break Stephanie and me up. Afterwards, we quickly gathered the children and went inside to meet Sister Claire. I introduced Mary and the children to Sister Claire; she offered us some coffee, milk, and cookies. We talked for a long time of how Mary and I met, and a short history of our lives. Stephanie told us about her life as a nun and how she enjoyed teaching.

Stephanie gave me her parent's telephone number and address. I asked her if it would be all right for me to talk with them before she did. I promised her I would speak to them gently and forgive them for what they had done. She told me she would not mention anything to them until after I had spoken to them. I also told her I would call her and give her a detailed account.

Before we left Stephanie gave our son and daughter two Holy Cards, each containing a picture of a saint. She had taken the Holy Cards from one of her habit pockets.

On our journey home, our son Tony said, "Hey Dad this saint on the Holy Card which Sister gave me looks just like you." Lisa said, "And the saint on mine looks just like Mom." Mary and I looked at the pictures, and the both saints did look like us.

When the kids fell asleep, Mary said, "I can see how she would pick out a saint that looks like you, but how could she pick one out that looks like me, she never met me before." I told Mary, "There are no coincidences and accidents in life. Everything happens for a reason. You can say it's the same way she told me in my dream to marry you."

The next morning I could not wait to contact the Mullens. I did not want to talk on the telephone, so I went to the Mullens' house. I went early in the morning so I could speak to Mrs. Mullen first. I believed Mr. Mullen would be at work. Afterwards I would speak to Mr. Mullen.

Mrs. Mullen came to the door, and recognized me immediately. Her first words were, "Tony, I thought you were dead." I explained to her as graciously as possible what had happened. She was shocked at what I told her. She had not been a part of her husband's scheme.

She was very angry and upset at her husband. She said, "Tony, I am so sorry for what he did to you. I thought he loved you as I did. How could he do this to you and to Stephanie? He kept this to himself all of these years. How could he live with himself? How could I live with him, Stephanie will never forgive him."

I told her, "I have spoken to Stephanie, and she understands what he did and why." I also told Mrs. Mullen that her husband only wanted the best for Stephanie, and he did what he thought was the right thing to do. I told her it was wrong what he did, but he had good intentions. Mrs. Mullen said, "Tony you are all that I thought you were. How can you feel about him the way you do after what he did to you and Stephanie?"

I also told her my wish for Stephanie, and her wish for me was that we both find happiness in our lives. I believe Stephanie is happy with her life the way it is, and I am happy with mine. I tried to convey that same feeling to her when I saw her yesterday. I believe *one should not take away one's hopes and dreams - it may be all they have to hold on.*"

Mrs. Mullen hugged me and asked me, 'What do I tell my husband." I told her, "I am going to speak to your husband later on in the day." I also told her, "Please try to forgive him for what he did, he thought he was doing the best thing for his daughter." I also told her, *"Un-forgiveness is like a heavy burden; it's like housing bitterness and hatred and will eventually wear you down."*

Mrs. Mullen told me she was going to call Stephanie and talk to her. I asked her if she would not talk to her husband until after I have spoken to him. She agreed.

Mrs. Mullen offered me some coffee and some of my favorite cookies. We talked about both of our lives and our relatives. Mrs. Mullen told me she believed that Stephanie and I would have made a wonderful life for each other. She also stated her and her husband dreamed of having many grandchildren.

I drove to Mr. Mullen's company, which was called Steph Dynamics, located in Wayne, New Jersey. When I saw the company name I thought to myself, how could I have not guessed his company's name when I was trying to locate him. He must love Stephanie very much, he names everything after her. To him, I think she is still his little girl.

The complex was huge, and judging by the number of cars in the parking lot, he must have over one hundred employees. I entered into a very nice office area, where I was greeted by a secretary. After greetings, she asked me who I wanted to see. I told her Mr. Mullen. She asked for my name, and I told her to tell Mr. Mullen it's an old friend. Her reply was, "I need a name sir." I told her, "Just tell him it's the proprietor from The Herera Industries."

I walked into the office, and Mr. Mullen almost fainted when he recognized me. He had heard of the Herera Industries, but he never connected it to me. He said, "Tony!" I extended my hand to greet him, and responded, "Mr. Mullen, glad to see you."

He said, "I did not know you were affiliated with the Herera Industries." I told him that I was, but I was not here regarding business. I came right out and told him I went and visited Sister Claire this past Sunday. His mouth was opened and had another surprised look about him.

I asked him, "Did you think we would never find out about this?" He said, "I was hoping you would not." My response was, "Life is full of many surprises." My next question was, "Why did you do such a thing?" He simply stated, "I thought Stephanie could find someone much better than you." My response was, "You mean a non-Hispanic." He said, "That's correct."

I told him, "I thought the world of you, and I had a lot of respect for you. I also thought you liked me." He did not respond. I continued, "Not only did you hurt me, you hurt Stephanie and you hurt your wife." He said, "What do you mean my wife?" I told him I had visited her this morning, and we had a nice conversation." He blurted out, "Oh my God."

I assured him that his wife was a bit shocked at first, but after our conversation she decided she might forgive you. Sister Claire was also upset at first, but she is gradually accepting this very unpleasant incident you placed on all of us.

I further told him, "I suggest you speak to both of them, and perhaps admit you have made a big mistake, and apologize to them." His response was. "What about you, how do you feel?" I said, "I care about Sister Claire and I care about your wife, they are both wonderful people and they did not deserve what you have done to them. Now it's up to you to do the rest, it's up to you help them get over it." I gave him my business card and departed.

Mr. Mullen left immediately for his home. Upon his arrival he was greeted by his wife, who was very upset. She said to him, "How could you do this. I thought I knew you. You deceived me and our daughter. Lucky for you Tony came over this morning and straightened things out; otherwise I might never forgive you for what you have done."

Mr. Mullen asked his wife, "What did Tony tell you?" Mrs. Mullen replied, "Tony told me you did what you thought was right for our daughter, you had good intentions, but I know it was a terrible thing you did. Tony tried to justify your mistake by telling me everything worked out for the best. He told me Stephanie is happy with her life as it is, and Tony is happy with his."

Mr. Mullen admitted he had made a big mistake, and asked his wife for forgiveness.

He told her, "I was all wrong about Tony. He is much more than I expected." Mrs. Mullen replied, "He made me feel comfortable with the blunder you pulled, and told me to forgive you. He also spoke to Stephanie and helped her see the best of this situation."

Mr. Mullen hugged his wife and told her he loved her. She replied, "It will take time for me to get over this."

I called Stephanie, as I had promised, and told her of the conversations I had with her parents. Stephanie thanked me and told me she was coming to Jersey to visit her parents on Saturday.

That evening I told Mary of the conversations I had with both Mr. Mullen and Mrs. Mullen. Mary's reply was, "I wish I could have seen his face when he first saw you." I also told her I had called Sister Claire and gave her an account of the conversations I had with her parents. I further told Mary that Sister Claire was coming to New Jersey to visit her parents this weekend. Mary asked, "Is Sister Claire coming to visit us?" I said, "No."

Several days later Sister Claire spoke to her Mother Superior. Sister Claire told her the story of what had happened to us. Afterwards, Mother Superior asked Sister Claire, "How do you feel about Tony?" Sister Claire responded, "I am happy that he is alive, and I am happy for the way his life turned out."

Mother Superior asked, "How does your heart feel about him?" Sister Claire said, "Regarding my personal feeling, in my heart I love him. My love for him is the same kind of love a sister has for her brother. I have a duty to my vow and a duty to my God, and I will keep the love I have for Tony in that perspective."

That weekend Sister Claire spoke to her mother and father. She told her father, "Dad, what you did was a very terrible thing. You misjudged Tony, you allowed your prejudices to make a bad decision, and you hurt people. I spoke to Mom and we both can live with your mistake, but I think you really hurt Tony. He loved you like a father and you turned on him. What are you going to do about it?" Her father said, 'What do you want me to do?" Sister Claire said, "Mom and I think you should apologize to him." He responded, "It's going to be hard for me to do that, but I will try."

Mr. Mullen called me and asked if we could have lunch during the week. I told him I was going on a business trip, but upon my return I would call him for a luncheon date. I was going to the NASA Space Center to meet with the engineers of the space program. I was granted the Heat Shield Contract I had applied for, and was to give them a presentation on my heat shields.

In my invitation, I was told that they were very much impressed with the outcome of the heat tests. They had received a written report from NASA Ames International Heating Facility. The heating facility was so amazed with the test results that they retested the heat shield three times, after each test the shield became more resilient to heat.

My trip to NASA would take three days, during that time my competitors were advised they were not awarded the contract. Through the Freedom of Information Act, every competitor could obtain the name of the company to whom the contract was awarded.

Upon my return I called Mr. Mullen and arranged for us to meet. At our meeting, Mr. Mullen's first words to me were, "Tony, I made a big mistake about you. I don't know much about you, but what you did for my wife and our relationship means a lot to me." I asked, "What do you mean?" Mr. Mullen said, "The way you tried to justify what I did, has saved my relationship with my wife and daughter, and I am most grateful to you. I was wrong in what I did, and I want to apologize for what I have done."

While we were eating, Mr. Mullen asked about my company. He stated he had heard about Herera Industries, but was not sure of exactly what it did. I told him we had some small government contracts, and the nature of our business. He told me his company provided similar services.

I asked him if he had applied for the Heat Shield Government Contract, and he-replied he did, and had just received notice he had not been selected. I asked him if he knew who had received the contact, and his reply was, "No, I haven't received any word on who was granted the contract."

Mr. Mullen continued, "I have applied for several small government contracts, and if I get them, which I am sure I will, those small contracts will keep my company operating at full capacity for at least seven more years."

We talked about our personal lives. I updated him on my education and my family life. Afterwards we parted. I felt he was sincere in his apology. I did not want to tell him my company had been granted the Heat Shield Contract, because I did not feel it was the right time.

I had also put in for several small government contracts. I put in for them just in case I would not get the Heat Shield Contract. If I had not gotten the Heat Shield Contract, the smaller contracts would keep my company alive for several years. I believe Mr. Mullen had the same idea. For his sake, I hoped he got some of those contracts he had applied for.

Mr. Mullen was notified that he was not granted any of the contracts he had applied for. This meant he would have to lay off most of his employees, and possibly even close the entire company. He was devastated.

Mr. Mullen did make inquiries to whom the government contracts he had applied for were granted. He was surprised when he discovered that Herera Industries was granted the Heat Shield Contract and every contract his company put in for.

He thought, "Is Tony trying to undermine my company? Was he getting back at me for what I did to him and Stephanie?" He became furious.

Fortunately, if he had to, he could sell the building and his equipment. This would give him enough money to support him and his wife for the rest of their lives, but it would break his heart to give up his business, which he loved, and lay off all his employees, many whom had become his close friends.

That evening he told his wife of his thoughts. Mrs. Mullen replied, "I have confidence in Tony. I don't believe he would do that to you, or anyone else. I am sure there is an explanation, why don't you talk to him."

Mr. Mullen responded, "I feel this way because I have made inquiries on his company, and they have a small location and a few employees. They will never be able to fulfill the Heat Shield Contract. I would be surprised if he could fulfill the small contracts he was awarded."

Mrs. Mullen said, "Perhaps he has intentions of subcontracting some of the work to other companies, maybe even you." He replied, "I would never accept that from him." Mrs. Mullen stated, "You have not changed, even though you apologized to him, you still hold prejudices toward him. What will it take to make you change? He doesn't feel that way about you. You would choose to close the business you love to spite him."

That evening Jay and Ann visited our home. I told them that Stephanie was alive, and that she had become a nun. I told him of what Mr. Mullen had done to break us up. They could not believe that he would do such a thing. Ann stated, "He went as far as getting a grave and putting up a false gravestone, what a monster."

I spoke to Jay about becoming a business partner; after all he was the big financier behind my company. He had always given me the loans I needed, and sound financial advice. I also spoke to him about not being able to fulfill the contracts, and perhaps not being able to meet some of the required deadlines on the smaller contracts.

I told him my idea was to subcontract some of the work. Jay's gut feeling was that when it comes to sensitive contracts, such as the government contracts, subcontracting might bring down the quality of product the Herera Industry has been providing. Jay said, "Tony your company is known for producing a very good product, do you want to lose that reputation?"

I told Jay, "I am aware of that, but how could I possibly meet the deadlines required, and at the same time put out the best product. I don't have the space or the manpower."

Mary suggested that subcontracting would be okay if the right subcontractor was selected and a close watch was kept on their progress. Jay and I agreed to what Mary had stated. I told Jay I would start visiting other similar companies, in an attempt to recruit the right one to help us meet our goals.

Before they left Jay told me he would consider my partnership offer and get back to me later during the week.

I started visiting other companies in the same business. I saw two that fitted the profile I was looking for, and I told them I would get back to them regarding my decision. My last stop was Steph Dynamics.

I walked into Mr. Mullen's office, and I started by telling him my company was the recipient of some government contracts. Mr. Mullen interrupted and said, "Tony I am aware that you have been granted the Shield Contract and several other government contracts, the same ones I have applied for."

I responded, "I was not aware that we have applied for the same contracts. How is that going to affect your company?" He said, "It's going to destroy us." I told him I was sorry that happened, and that I was visiting other companies in the same business in order to recruit one to subcontract some of my work to them.

Mr. Mullen asked, "You were not aware that you had applied for the same contracts I applied for?" I asked him, "How would I know what contracts you applied for?" I further told him, "I applied for all contracts in my line of business. Hoping to get a few of them so I can keep my company going. I believe you did the same thing. I got the contracts because I have a reputation of putting out a very good product."

Mr. Mullen said, "Tony, I have a gut feeling you were out to destroy my company, and congratulations you have." I replied, "Mr. Mullen, I am sorry you feel that way, but the truth is I would not do that to you or anyone else."

I asked Mr. Mullen, "What are you going to do with your business?" He replied, "I have no choice. I have to sell the building, sell all of the equipment, and lay off all of my employees."

I asked him, "Would subcontracting some of my work help?" He replied, "Subtracting would not help because I have too many employees, and I am not ready to take any charity work."

I told him, "Could you work out a figure and get back to me on a price for the building and the equipment?" His remark was, "I don't think you can afford it." I said, "Just let me know." I thanked him, went to shake his hand, which he did not accept, so I left.

That evening I called Jay and he was under the same impression I was, that buying the building and the equipment would be too expensive. I then came up with the idea of including Mr. Mullen in our partnership. Jay's response was, "You would consider that after what he did to you and Stephanie, and after he refused to shake your hand, are you crazy?"

That same evening Mr. Mullen told Mrs. Mullen of the conversation we had during the day. Mrs. Mullen told her husband that he was very hard on me, and that he had no right to treat me the way he did. She told him, "I think you still feel Tony was out to destroy you and you are wrong."

Next morning I met with Mr. Mullen. His first words were, "I don't recall you setting up a meeting with me." I told him, "I did not set up meeting with you, but I have an offer for you." I told him, "I want you be become a partner in my company. The company will be made up of three owners. You will hold thirty percent of the company, Mr. Pearlman will hold the other thirty percent, and I will hold forty percent."

He said, "Do you mean Mr. Pearlman from the Pearlman Group, the financier?" I said, "That's correct." I continued, "Mr. Pearlman and I will pay you for the two thirds of your building, and two thirds of your equipment. Therefore, everyone partnered in the company owns it. Mr. Pearlman runs the financial aspect of the company, and you run the production end of it. That is you will still supervise all of the employees. However, there will be strict guidelines. I will run the research and development aspects of the company. We can discuss it further if you are interested. I have asked Mr. Pearlman to meet with us, he should be here shortly. Then we can draw up a contract."

Mr. Mullen was shocked. He stuttered his approval. Jay arrived and we sat down and began to draw up the contract. We ordered lunch in so we could continue to work. At the end of the day, we had our contract and all were pleased.

Mr. Mullen would continue to work in the company he loved, and keep all of his employees. He would continue to be their leader as before. He was also getting a lump sum of money that would keep him financially sound for the rest of his life. He received more than he had ever hoped for.

Jay would have his own little financial investment toy he always wanted. I knew he did it for me, but I would make sure he would not be sorry for it. Furthermore, I thought he would enjoy it.

I had a company that would fulfill all the government contracts that had been awarded to me. I would see to it that best products would be produced from it, and make a good effort to make the company grow. I felt it was a great beginning.

That evening Jay, Ann, Mary and I went out to dinner to celebrate. Ann said, "Tony, I think Mr. Mullen ought to kiss the ground you walk on for what you have done for him." Mr. Mullen also took his wife out to dinner, and said to her, "I don't deserve what Tony has done for me. He has given me more money than I need, he has allowed me to continue to keep my company, and has given me thirty percent of this new company. I have been so wrong about him, I feel like a heel. I never gave him a chance. Why would he do such a thing?" Mrs. Mullen told him, "He likes you, he respects you, and he knows more about you than you know about yourself.

He sees the goodness that lies deep within you. He also has faith in you and knows that you will do your best to make the company grow."

Mr. Mullen responded, "I will make it up to him, I will try my best to make this company very successful, and I will try to be the friend he thinks I am." Mrs. Mullen replied, "All you have to do is your best. Tony knows where your heart is."

The two companies were combined, and the merger went smoothly. Offices were set up for the three partners. The place was well lit, clean and a pleasure to be in. We tried to make the work environment as pleasant as possible.

The employees received their same salaries, but would be receiving regular raises as the company grew and got more settled.

Inspectors from NASA came to see and inspect the premises. They were very much impressed with the equipment and our operation. They were mostly impressed with the products they received.

The Herera Industries would celebrate the Christmas holidays by holding a Christmas dinner, a week before Christmas, at the Bow and Arrow. At the dinner all the employees were given a week's salary as a bonus.

Family members of the administrators would also attend; Sister Claire could not attend, due to her very busy school schedule, and her religious commitments. She was seen by members of her family only on special occasions.

Our children only saw her on two occasions, and knew her only as Sister Claire, the daughter of the Mullens.

Jay would work at the company two to three days per week, to oversee company fiscal matters. The salary he received from the company was strictly used to pay off his investment. That is the one third of the cost for the purchase of the building and the equipment, which was given to Mr. Mullen.

Jay still worked for his father, and used that salary for his day-to-day expenses. I, on the other hand had to use my salary to pay for my day-to-day expenses, and to also pay for my part of the company investment. I had to financially struggle a bit for several years, but I knew it would be well worth it.

One day I was cleaning out my cabinet, which housed memorabilia I had collected for many years. In an old envelope I came across the rosary beads my mom had given to me at my confirmation, the ones I told Stephanie I would give her when we got married. The ones I had inscribed with her name – Stephanie Mullen.

I talked to Mary about the rosary beads, and told her the story behind them and how I tried to give them to Stephanie many years ago. Mary and I agreed that they should be given to Sister Claire, especially when they had her name on them.

Mary came up with the idea that if she would give the beads to Sister, Mary believed Sister would be more likely to accept them from her. Mary placed them in a small box, wrapped the box, and tied a cute little red bow on it.

Mary placed a greeting card in a larger mailing envelope with the box. She wrote on the card: Sister Claire, Tony and I came across these rosary beads, the ones which were given to him by his mother. He told me the story behind the beads. Please accept them as a special gift from us, we know you will use them. Mary signed the card Mary and Tony.

Several days later we received a thank you note from Sister Claire. The card read, "I immediately recognized the rosary beads, and I thank the both of you for being so considerate. I will put them to good use and I will pray for you and your family." It was signed Sister Claire.

CHAPTER TEN

"Better Days Are Coming"

✸ One Saturday evening, Mary, the kids and I were invited to dine at the Mullens'. It was just the Mullens, Mary, our children and me. Sister Claire, as usual, was not present. Mrs. Mullen made her special chocolate chip cookies. Mary loved the cookies and asked Mrs. Mullen for her recipe, which she was proud to provide.

After we left Mrs. Mullen said to Mr. Mullen, "I think Tony loves her very much." Mr. Mullen asked his wife, "Why did you mention that." She replied, "Because when he broke the cookie in half, he gave the bigger half to Mary. That is what he would do when he shared his cookie with Stephanie."

Mr. Mullen said to his wife. "That could have been Stephanie sitting next to him, and those could have been our grandchildren. What a mistake I made." Mrs. Mullen replied, *"Don't be so hard on yourself what you did is water under the bridge, it has passed and will never pass under the same bridge again."* Mr. Mullen had a few tears in his eyes. It was the first time he ever showed his real feeling towards Tony.

The Herera Industries became very successful. Tony had finally paid off his initial investment debt, and was able to reinvest into the company. Mr. Mullen and Jay also invested their profit back into the company.

Jay enjoyed being part of the company and would devote more time to it. He also spent more time with his friend Tony.

The company was still working on government contracts. Government contracts do not last forever, so the company began to make and sell other products to private industries. Eventually selling to the private sector became more and more lucrative and the company profits increased. It also brought more stability to the company.

Years went by and out of nowhere my mother took ill, and died from heart failure three days later. She was buried next to my grandfather.

That evening I thought about both of them, and I started going through my grandfather's letters. Lisa and Tony entered the room and started reading the letters. I told them I was brought up by following the words of wisdom that are written on these letters.

Your mother and I tried to raise you the same way I was raised, and your mother and I, when we pass away, requested that the both of you take these letters and try to raise your children the same way.

Mary told them, "The words of wisdom on these letters will never be out-dated, and will be appropriate for generations to come. Remember as Tony's grandfather wrote in one of these letters, *much of your growth will come through hardships and many challenges. You have to embrace them and know that you will be better, stronger and wiser because of them.*"

Mrs. Mullen passed away from heart failure, and several months later Mr. Mullen also died. Shortly after Mr. Mullen's death, Jay, Ann, Mary and I met in Daniel Monahan's office. He was the attorney who represented Mr. Mullen..

At this meeting, Mr. Mullen's attorney told Jay and me that the Mullen share of the Herera Industries was turned over to a secret account. The benefactor was to remain anonymous. All of Mr. Mullen's profits would go into this secret account.

Any decisions on company matters, which would have been made on the part of Mr. Mullen, would be passed on to Mr. Herera. In other words, I would be acting on the part of Mr. Mullen.

I asked the attorney if Mr. Mullen's daughter had been consulted in these affairs, and the attorney responded that she had been, and was very instrumental in its preparations.

I also asked him what happened to the Mullen estate, and the attorney responded that $1,000,000.00 of the estate went to Sister Claire's order.

He also mentioned that Sister Claire is now Mother Superior of her order. He further mentioned that the Mullen house and furniture were sold and the money was given to charity.

After the meeting Jay, Ann, Mary and I went to dine. We talked about who this secret partner might be. We came up with the idea that perhaps Sister Claire had turned over her father's thirty percent of the company to her order. Her order, which is not business-oriented, nor perhaps is allowed to hold investments in the private sector, made a sound decision. That is to have the company continue to run as it is, and use the profits for the order. This was all speculation on our part.

Our children grew up quickly; Lisa was attending New York University and pursuing a Master's Degree in Business Administration. Tony had graduated Rutgers Law School and was preparing for his bar examination.

Jay and Ann's son John was also attending New York University and was pursuing a Master's Degree in Business Administration. He was following in his father's and grandfather's footsteps. He too would soon be working for the Pearlman Group. Their daughter Melissa had graduated William Paterson College, and was pursuing a teaching career.

Many years later Mary developed cancer and had several cancer operations which were followed up chemotherapy. Finally she was given days to live. I stayed with her at the hospital; I wanted to be there for her when her final day came.

The day she died she thanked me for being a wonderful husband. She told me she was very proud of me and our children. She stated, "Tony you are the best thing that has ever happened to me, and I want to thank you for being a wonderful husband and a good father. You have made me very happy."

I told her, "Mary you have made our marriage what it is, I want to thank you for what you have done, you are the true leader of what we have accomplished together." I told her that I loved her very much.

The nurse came in to give her medication. I went to the cafeteria to get a cup of coffee, and when I returned she had passed away. I looked up and said, "Lord, You know I wanted to be here for her when her time came, why couldn't You have waited a few more minutes?"

Hospital stays are very unpleasant, but today was a special day. As I lay in my bed I closed my eyes and spoke to the Lord. I told Him that this might be the last time I am able to speak to Him while I am here on earth. "I just want to thank You for Mary, my children, all of my family and everything else You have given to me. I hope that You are happy with what I have done with all of the gifts You gave to me, and how I used them to help others. If I have made any mistakes, which I know I have, please forgive me and be merciful to me."

A voice responded, and said, "Tony, you have been a good and faithful person. It sounded like Sister Claire's voice. I opened my eyes I saw her sitting on a chair. I said to her, "Sister Claire thanks for visiting me." Sister replied, "Tony, how could I have not visited you." I asked her, "Sister, can I address and talk to you as Stephanie for a few minutes?" She stated, "Tony you know me well enough, of course you can."

I told her, "Stephanie, as you know very well, when I first met you I fell deeply in love with you. That love lasted until you gave me permission to love and marry Mary. Stephanie, I truly loved Mary and treated her as I would have treated you. Then, after all those years of thinking you were dead you came back into my life. From that day on my heart leaped with joy, and I felt about you the same way I felt when I first met you. However, I had a commitment to Mary, a vow to her which I had to keep.

I also, at one time, broke her heart and I promised her I would never hurt her again. So, in order to keep my commitment to her, I had to suppress that love that had once again been rekindled for you.

Stephanie, I am truly sorry of what happened to our love. Please forgive me for speaking to you today from my heart. Tell me Steph, did I do the right thing?"

Stephanie replied, "Tony, of course you did the right thing. The marriage commitment you made to Mary was one that was personally blessed by Jesus, and you have kept that commitment and you will be rewarded for it. *It is our sorrows that keep us human.*"

I thanked her and asked her to pray for me. She responded, "Tony I have been praying for you and your family for years, and I will continue to do so." I thanked her again. Stephanie then squeezed my hand tightly and kissed the back of it.

Sister Claire left the room, and my two children entered and asked if I needed anything or if there was anything they could do for me. I told them, "I love you very much, and your mother and I are very proud of what you have become. It was the two of you and your mom which made our life so wonderful. *Life goes on, and life is very precious. It's what we do with our life which is most important. What you can do for me is to try to live a good life, be kind and generous to others by reaching out to as many people as you can,* and most importantly be happy for mom and I because we will be together in a better place." I kissed and hugged them both before they left the room. Tony passed away a short time afterwards.

Tony and Lisa were looking through their father's personal belongings for some old photographs to display at the funeral parlor, when Lisa found her father's Eastside High School yearbook. Right on the first page she saw and said to her brother, "Hey Tony, just listen to what was written in Dad's year book. 'Tony, our love was a flame meant to be before we were born. We both lit that flame when we first met. Let's keep it burning for all eternity.' It's signed Forever yours, Stephanie."

Tony responded, "Listen to the postcard I found, 'Tony, I began to miss you the moment you left. I cannot wait until we graduate so we can be together forever,' and it's signed Forever yours, Stephanie."

Tony said to Lisa, "Who in the world is Stephanie?" Lisa responded, "It's obvious that she was and old girlfriend." Tony stated, "I thought that Mom was Dad's only girlfriend." Lisa said, "We'll never know."

The funeral Mass was held at Tony's old church, St. Joseph's Church located on Market Street in Paterson, N.J. It was well attended. Sister Claire sat near to the Herera family, and all through the service she kept praying her rosary beads.

Tony was buried next to his wife Mary, very close to his mother, his grandfather, and his sister Lucy. The internment was attended by family members; Jay and Ann, most of the employees of The Herera Industries, and Sister Claire.

After the graveside service, all were invited to the Brownstone for the repasts. Tony and Lisa saw Sister Claire drop her rosary beads as she was walking towards her car.

Tony picked up the beads and called out to Sister. He looked at the beads to admire their beauty, and read the name inscribed on them – Stephanie Mullen.

Tony asked sister if she was Stephanie Mullen. Sister replied, "Yes." At this time Lisa caught up to the both of them. Lisa had heard Sister replied that she was Stephanie Mullen. Lisa asked sister if she dated her father. Sister replied that she did. Lisa told her that she and her brother had found her father's yearbook and a postcard written by her to their father.

Lisa asked, "It appeared that the two of you were very much in love." Sister Claire replied, "Your father and I were very much in love." Lisa then asked, "What happened"? Sister Claire replied, "God had other plans for the both of us."

Sister went to her car, started the motor, and thought to herself. "Tony loved me very much, and I loved him with all my heart and I still do." Tears fell from her eyes.

Three months later Lisa and Tony received a letter from Daniel Monahan, the Mullen family attorney. The letter asked them to come to his office. At the office, Mr. Monahan told them Sister Claire had passed away, and that she, who is also known as Stephanie Mullen, set up a secret account many years ago for them. They now hold thirty more percent of the Herera Industries, and a savings account worth over thirty two million dollars that has accumulated over the years.

Lisa asked Mr. Monahan, "Why would Sister Claire do that for us?" Mr. Monahan responded, "Frankly, I don't know."

After a Herera Industries company meeting, Tony and Lisa, who now own seventy percent of the company, spoke to Jay. Tony asked Jay, "Do you know why Sister Claire would leave her father's shares of the company to us?" Jay said, "I have a pretty good idea." Jay began to tell them about the wonderful love relationship between their father and Stephanie, and what happened to that relationship.